PONIES IN PERIL

DIANA PULLEIN-THOMPSON

AN ARMADA ORIGINAL

Ponies in Peril was first published in Armada in 1979 by
Fontana Paperbacks,
14 St. James's Place, London SW1A 1PS

© Diana Pullein-Thompson 1979

Printed in Great Britain by
Love & Malcomson Ltd., Brighton Road,

Redhill, Surrey.

CONTENTS

To Benedict and
Joanna with love

PATIENCE

JIGSAW

SOLITAIRE

PING PONG

TIDDLYWINKS

HOPSCOTCH

CHAPTER ONE

ALL GOING FOR MEAT

"They're as wild as hawks," said Jake, sliding from his saddle. "See them? Beauties, though, aren't they?"

We looked across the meadow to the trees where six four and five-year-old ponies stood swishing their long tails against the flies.

"And all going for meat," added our friend, opening the gate. "It's a crying shame."

"But why?" I asked. "Couldn't they be sold to good homes?"

"Money," replied Jake grimly. "Love of money is at the root of all evil—that's from the Holy Bible, isn't it?"

"Yes, yes, I'm sure," replied my brother, dismounting to lead Mimosa through the gate.

"Thought you were educated, Fergie," teased Jake. "Thought you would give us chapter and verse."

"Not from the Bible," said my brother. "I'm not doing theology or R.I. for 'O' Level. But tell us the story again. Dylan Jones has died. Right?"

"Right," agreed Jake.

"And his heirs care nothing for the farm or the animals. They just want to settle the estate, sell up as soon as posisible, and pocket the cash, after taxes have been paid."

"Nicely put," said Jake, lighting a cigarette.

"And it's quickest to sell the ponies for meat—for France, I suppose," said Fergie, a crease appearing above his dark brows which almost met above his fine straight nose.

"An offer has been made—six hundred pounds," said Jake, starting to lead his bay, Bullfinch, across the field towards the trees. "It's not a lot; maybe you could get

9

double that if the ponies were broken and schooled, but who's going to do that? Labour here's expensive and it takes a good six weeks to break an ordinary pony, let alone a wild bunch like this lot. They haven't been handled since they were foals."

"What about us?" I asked in a rush.

"Us?" echoed Jake.

"Fergie and me?"

"Well, if you've got six hundred pounds to spare . . ."

"We haven't, that's the short answer," said my brother.

By now we could see the ponies clearly, as they turned to stare at us with their pointed ears pricked and their eyes shining. There were two greys, one bay, a skewbald, a dun and a dark brown. Their heights varied from around 11.3 up to 13.3 hands high.

"The larger ones have a streak of Arab, you can see it in their heads and the way they carry their tails," said Jake. "If they were registered they would have fetched more, but old Dylan never bothered with that sort of thing—hated paperwork."

"He bred them himself?" asked Fergie.

"Yes, he had a stallion running with his mares for years. Very haphazard it was. He liked things natural. None of this new-fangled stuff," said Jake. "The mention of factory farming was enough to bring on a heart attack. But now, of course, he's left his muddle for someone else to sort out."

As we drew near, the ponies turned, and, with several loud snorts, set off across the meadow at full gallop, their tails streaming out behind them.

"Just think of all that beauty carved up and hanging in the butchers' shops in France," said Jake.

"Or put into tins as stewing steak," added Fergie.

"We've got to save them," I insisted. "Dad can loan us the money."

"He's got to buy a new engine for the mini-bus, remember?" said Fergie. "Six hundred pounds is quite a lot of money, more than half of one thousand pounds."

"And they won't be easy to break," added Jake. "That's not going to be a walkover. You've got to start right at the very beginning. It will take time."

"We could pay Dad back with interest—even make a profit in the end," I argued.

"*If* things work out," said Fergie.

The ponies had stopped and were standing in a little huddle like frightened sheep, staring at us. They all had fine, small heads with wide cheeks and long forelocks and manes.

"Three geldings and three mares," said Jake. "And pretty as a picture. But there it is, there are more unbroken animals around than the public needs. It's like mongrel dogs, isn't it? They're being destroyed in their hundreds while the pedigree ones fetch forty or fifty pounds apiece. It doesn't make sense to my way of thinking. I'd rather have a mongrel, myself. Sharper, they are, and stronger than most of the inbred show specimens."

We mounted our ponies and rode back across the field into Shropshire with the sun in our eyes and a gentle breeze blowing across from the wilder parts of Wales.

"I shall ask Dad after he's eaten supper when he's feeling good," I insisted.

"You won't get anywhere," said Fergie.

"There's no harm in asking," put in Jake. "Now, who's going to do the gate?"

Riding back across the top of Offa's Dyke, Fergie said, "Ponies in Peril. That makes a good headline, doesn't it? Think of it in black print across the top of a newspaper. We must launch an appeal, like people trying to save the country's heritage—works of art and so on. Well, why are you grinning, Jake? What's wrong with that?"

"You're thinking big, aren't you, and there's only a week to go," said our friend. "I'll do my best, mind. I'll have a word with Dylan's son, Emlyn; he's a strange bloke, but not without some goodness in him. I'll tell him you're upset. He doesn't like to think of children being

11

miserable—funny thing that. He cares so much for kids but animals mean nothing to him."

"We're not children," said Fergie. "I'll soon be fifteen and Sandy's thirteen. A few years back and I could have been at work if I chose to leave school."

"Well, teenagers haven't the best reputation amongst adults, have they?" asked Jake. "You've got to use your nous when you're asking a favour, you know. A little diplomacy can work wonders if you want a stay of execution."

"Young people—*nice* young people—then," suggested my brother. "You can't call me a child now that I'm as tall as you."

"Just leave it to me," said Jake, stubbing out a cigarette. "How about a canter?"

CHAPTER TWO

I WOULDN'T WANT ONE FOR MY KIDDIES

"No, I'm sorry. I'm skint," said Dad, smiling blandly. "I wish I could help, but what with the income-tax man and the electricity bill and the new engine for the bus . . . Well, you know the story. Too many little brown envelopes falling on the doormat."

"Don't look at me," pleaded our mother, pushing back her chair. "I can't lay my hands on six hundred pounds, not in these days of wicked inflation. Anyone want second helpings?"

She walked across our warm farmhouse kitchen to the *Aga* stove, looking younger than her forty-odd years in jeans and a high-necked, dark blue sweater with darned elbows. Leerie, our tri-coloured, rough-coated collie followed her hopefully. "I don't mean *you*," she added, patting him.

"Yes, please," said Fergie.

"Bring your plate across then," said Mum. "Your legs are younger than mine."

Soon we had finished supper and washed up and then we went to my brother's bedroom, which was long and low and looked out on a hill which rose like a camel's hump to meet the wide Shropshire sky. Sitting on the divan bed, we made plans, writing down all our ideas on a piece of paper. And the next day at school we carried out the first of these. After meeting by the telephone during break, we dialled the number of the local newspaper, asked for the Reporters' Desk and then spoke to a young woman with a Welsh accent.

Fergie explained the position. "We thought it would make a story, you know, *campaign to save ponies from the butchers' knives,* that sort of thing," he finished a little breathlessly.

"We only need to borrow six hundred pounds and we are away," I added, having taken the phone. "We can break them in, find them good homes, and then pay back the loan."

"Steady," said the reporter, "you're going too fast. You're telescoping things. Where are you? And where are the ponies? If I'm to make a story out of this I must bring along a photographer. It needs a picture."

I gave her our address and said we could guide her to the ponies' field, and then Fergie took back the phone. "Can you ride?" he asked, and she must have said no because then he said that it was quite a walk and that she'd need tough shoes.

I hissed, "Make it Saturday morning!"

And he said: "I'm afraid we are only free weekends. We're still at school and the evenings are getting a bit dark for photographs."

Then she must have asked him to tell the story again, because he went very slowly through all the events, starting with the death of Dylan Jones and finishing with a vivid description of the six ponies galloping across the meadows with their tails streaming out behind them. "They're all by the same stallion—what did you say? No, I mean they all have the same father, a fine Welsh pony. All right, Saturday at ten o'clock. Fine, thank you very much. See you then. 'Bye."

He put down the receiver. "Next time, we draw lots or toss up to decide who does the talking, if you refuse to accept that I should because I'm the eldest," he said, glaring. "It's so unbusinesslike when we snatch the phone from each other."

"You weren't giving the practical details, but harping on the emotional guff," I complained. "The most important fact is that we need six hundred pounds."

"But there's got to be a build-up. Reporters always want a bit of colour," argued Fergie.

Then the bell went, so we had to go into school again.

Saturday dawned wet, and we wondered how the reporter would manage, trekking across the rough hillside in pouring rain. Dad said the light was too bad for photographs, and Mum said we wouldn't look our best in our tatty old mackintoshes.

"But we should seem poor," insisted Fergie. "I mean we *are* poor, we must be if we can't raise six hundred pounds in an emergency."

Dad said we could if it were a matter of life and death, because then he would sell the bullocks, and I made the obvious retort that it *was*, and Dad said he meant life and death for us, not another person's ponies. Then the front door bell rang and there was the reporter on the doorstep, blonde, beak-nosed, dressed in jeans, a blue anorak and clogs.

"Have a cup of coffee? How kind of you to come," said our mother in that order.

Sitting at our large kitchen table, the reporter brought out her notebook and we went through the whole story again over coffee.

"Now my photographer's a hardy guy who braves the rain and I see him outside this minute parking his car," she said as she finished the last sentence. "Isn't that perfect timing?" She put down her pencil.

"Fabulous, but I think we should lend you boots," suggested Fergie, looking disapprovingly at her clogs.

"In my car," she said. "I'm countrybred. I know about these things."

We gave the photographer a cup of coffee and then piled into his old Morris and set off up the hill to the farm which had belonged to Dylan Jones. We parked boldly in the yard and the rain started to clear as we trudged up the track along which we had ridden only three days earlier. The wind was in our faces and the hill was steep, and the photographer, a burly man in his forties, puffed.

15

"You must take up jogging, Geoff, be in the swing," teased Liz, the reporter, with the last of the rain dripping off her nose and running down the rear of the black sou'-wester which she had donned.

"Take up golf, more likely," said the photographer, wiping his moustache, which was the colour of a thorn hedge in winter. "How much further?"

"About a quarter of a mile," said Fergie, "but we'll soon be on the flat. We're coming to Wales now."

When we reached the crest of the hill we could see the ponies grazing with their manes and forelocks blown hither and thither by the wind, and their tails clamped tight between their legs.

"Wild as hawks," said Fergie, using Jake's idiom. "Heaven knows how we're going to catch them if we raise the money."

"Round them up," said Liz, "Wild West style."

"We're no use with lassoos," said Fergie, who was inclined to take jokes too seriously.

We came to the gate at last, and, as we opened it, the largest grey, who was standing alone, threw up his head and took us in with his large dark eyes.

"What are their names?" asked Liz.

"They haven't any," I said. "But their Dad was called Mastermind."

"You could call them Snooker and Snap, then, after other games, I suppose," suggested Liz. "Look, the sky's clearing. I can see a patch of blue."

"They're super," said Geoff. "But Lord knows how I'm going to get a picture. They look as nervous as hares and can probably move as fast."

"If we all go across the field they're bound to gallop off, but if one goes alone he might get quite near," I said.

Now all the ponies' heads were up, as they came closer together like frightened sheep.

"We'll stay here, quite still, keeping their attention while you tip-toe round on the right, with your camera at the

16

ready," suggested Liz. "When they spot you, they'll turn and look and you can take the photograph."

The skewbald was watching us intently, bright eyes shining through a chestnut and white forelock. She was prettily marked, mainly white, with golden patches on her back, flank and haunches and running down her legs. The dun gelding stood at her side, a stockier pony, the colour of wheat, with a darker mane and tail.

"They don't look as though they're all from the same sire," remarked Liz.

"Perhaps they weren't. Mr. Jones was not very organized, by all accounts," said Fergie. "There could have been a mistake."

The photographer edged closer, then took his camera from its case. The ponies turned their heads; the smaller grey let out a snort and in a trice they were all galloping away across the field.

"So much for your brilliant idea!" said Geoff with a grin. "Their hearing is fabulous. They heard the camera sliding out of the case. Incredible! Like gazelles, aren't they?"

"They're going up towards the corner. We might trap them there long enough to get a picture," suggested Fergie.

So we trudged across the field, our feet slipping in the mud as we neared the corner where the ponies had been fed from time to time. They were now standing in a bunch again, anxious-eyed, alert, watching our every move.

"Wary devils," said Geoff, snapping them. "Now you two," he gesticulated at Fergie and me. "Get as close to them as you can. We want you in the picture too."

We walked, we crawled. We stopped every few strides. We crept silently. We crooned, we talked in soothing tones, we sang lullabies, but each time we were within fifty yards or so the ponies moved off.

"Haven't you got your telescopic lens?" asked Liz, laughing.

"Not to worry," said the photographer, ignoring the quip. "We'll take you separately and then inset your faces.

It's quite easy. Come on, we've wasted enough time on these blighters. Heaven only knows how you're going to train them. I wouldn't want one for my kiddies."

As we trudged back across the field, a thin drizzle of rain fell softly like dew and the ground squelched under our feet. Reaching the gate at last, we heard hooves behind us and saw that the ponies were following us at a brisk trot.

"They're as curious as cattle," said Liz.

The dark brown mare was in the lead, moving near to the ground like a thoroughbred, closely followed by the tallest grey and then the little bay who had a white blaze running down his face, finishing in a trickle just above his nostrils. Then came the skewbald, looking like the joker in a pack, a little brash amongst the others and yet with a delicacy about her face which gave her an air of breeding. The dun trotted, his action higher than the others, as though he would be a fine pony in a governess cart, his head tougher, less clear-cut, with a rough-hewn, rock-like beauty about it. Last came the dapple grey, a bouncy dumpling sort of pony, with her winter coat already blurring her outline and a merry look in her eyes, as though she didn't take life very seriously.

We climbed the gate and stopped, and then the ponies stopped too, watching us warily.

"If we walk away, they'll probably come and look over the gate and then if you hide behind that gorse bush, like a wild-life photographer, you might get a picture," I suggested.

"Fair enough," said Geoff.

The ruse succeeded, and afterwards the photographer took a dozen pictures of us at home with our own ponies. He kept saying, "Look a little brighter. Can we have a smile, please," and "Cheer up, what's the trouble?" My brother and I both found it hard to pose for photographs. Annoyed with the freckles on my face and the wildness of my hairs, I always become gloomy, for I longed to be dark and romantic like an Italian princess instead of braw and Scottish. Lucky Fergie was Celtic in appearance, with Mummy's distinguished nose and high brow, his dark hair rising up to a sort of crest at the top of his head. But he had a silly idea that one of his shoulders was higher than the other and thought his neck ugly, so he also found it hard to smile when his face was being photographed.

Afterwards I said, "Well, we should be looking sad. After all, six ponies are about to be killed for meat."

"People are more likely to offer help to charming youngsters than surly ones," said Liz realistically. "The younger and sweeter you look the better."

The next evening Jake came round to say that Emlyn Jones had agreed to allow us another week. "But he wants you to know that you must arrange transport, and, worse still, the catching. I'll help, of course. You can use my truck, that's no problem."

"I've been talking to Dad," said Fergie. "And we've decided we can keep them in the barn. We can tame them more easily that way."

"*If* we raise the money," I put in. "We've thought about holding a little fête, but Dad thinks we would have to be a registered charity for that and there's so little time. So we've decided on a jumble sale. Anything to spare, Jake?"

"I'll see what the wife has," said our friend, who ran a pony-trekking centre as well as a cattle transport business. "She's got a wardrobe full of clothes she's grown out of, if you know what I mean. Have you told the newspaper girl?"

"Not about the jumble sale," said Fergie. "We've only just thought of that."

"Better ring her up then. You want a plug for it, don't you?" said Jake. "Mustn't miss any chance of publicity. And don't forget to make a few notices for the electricity poles—stick them on. By the time any official spots them the sale will be over."

"I don't see why they should object," I added. "It's all in a good cause."

19

Later we went round to a few neighbours, begging jumble. Apple-cheeked Mrs. Grundell found a lace handkerchief which had belonged to her mother. The Clays, a large family, who ran a bed and breakfast business as well as a farm, told us to call back, when, they assured us, they could produce ten pairs of outgrown shoes in good condition. An old man in a bungalow gave us two wooden candlesticks, and the local schoolmistress produced a block of writing paper with envelopes, three handkerchiefs, four tins of talcum powder, three cakes of scented soap and a bottle of ginger ale, which were all presents given to her by pupils at the end of term.

The next morning at school we rang Liz to tell her about the jumble sale and we booked the village hall in a neighbouring village with a population three times the size of our own. In the evening we wrote out notices advertising the sale, and the following morning we rose at six, took a hurricane lantern, and walked two miles, sticking them on telephone and electricity poles. They read as follows:

PONIES IN PERIL
A Jumble Sale is to be held
On Saturday September 18th
At the Village Hall,
Landorck-on-Clun, at 2.30 p.m.
In aid of the Campaign to Save
Six Ponies from Slaughter for
Human Consumption

CHAPTER THREE

SOMETHING'S *GOT* TO HAPPEN

The write-up appeared in the local paper on the following Saturday, big and bold with a photograph of the dark brown mare and the largest grey looking over the gate with the skewbald and dun in the background. A small picture of Fergie and I, encircled by a grey line, was inset in the top left-hand corner, and the whole piece was headed with the words *PONIES IN PERIL*. It read:

Fergus and Sandy Hamilton of Stanton-on-Clun are fighting to save six ponies from the knackers yard. They were the property of Mr. Dylan Jones of White Farm, Stanton-on-Clun, who died last month, and are now destined for the Continental meat market unless action is taken within two weeks.

"They're super ponies and far too good for sausages," said Sandy, aged 13, yesterday, "and we are going to raise heaven and hell to save them."

Fergus, 14, explained that they need a loan of six hundred pounds to allow them to buy them and break them in. "Once they are tamed and schooled," he said, "they will find homes easily enough. The trouble is that they're as wild as hawks."

The prospective buyers, a meat trading company, were unavailable for comment yesterday. A local farmer, Mr. J. H. Dawson, commented, "It's a crying shame that so many ponies are going abroad as meat. It will soon be impossible to buy an ordinary little pony, only the pedigree ones which fetch high prices. Something needs to be done before it's too late. I think Fergus and Sandy are doing a great job."

Part of that job is running a jumble sale to raise funds at the Village Hall, Landorck-on-Clun, at 2.30 pm on next Saturday, September 18th. Fergus says: "Anyone wishing to make us a loan to save the ponies should be refunded with interest once they are trained and saleable. We're not begging, simply asking for a little help. And any jumble should be delivered to us at Varley Farm, Stanton-on-Clun, by noon on Saturday next."

"Well, they've not done you too badly," remarked Dad, handing back the paper. "And Jake's put in a good word."

"But I never use adjectives like super," I complained. "That's pure invention."

"Och, reporters can't remember everything. You must allow them a wee bit of poetic licence now and then. It's not fair to quibble over little things when they've given you such a wide spread," argued our mother. "It's a fine picture, too. You mustn't be churlish."

"Liz makes it sound as though donors will be rewarded with interest when they are trained and saleable," said Fergie, who was much involved in studying English grammar for his exams. "But still it's wonderful publicity and I'm very pleased."

"You look keen but a bit wild," said Dad. "Sandy's hair could have done with a tidy-up."

"Now for jumble hunting. Come on! Where are the baskets?" I deliberately changed the subject, not wanting my looks to become a topic of conversation.

A few moments later, we set out in different directions through the village. It was one of those soft September days, when the air was damp and fragrant with the mellow scents of early autumn. The grass was still green and there were patches of blue in the watery grey sky; birds sang in the willows by the river, and Mrs. Grundell's speckled hens scratched industriously in the winding lane. A collie raised himself lazily from a sunny doorstep and barked at me, more from duty than fierceness. I loved our village, which

22

lay between two hills, more than any other place on earth. It had become part of me. Unplanned, it had grown as mole heaps and warrens grow, with little lanes threading their way between the cottages, not drawn in advance on paper but made by the feet of men. The great hills watched over it like sentinels, and everywhere there was a feeling of eternity which made everyday problems seem small in comparison with the profoundness of life itself.

My looks no longer mattered as I walked briskly over the bridge towards a grey farmhouse that stood halfway up a hill. Who could indeed care about a few freckles when the air was so fragrant with the scent of autumn and the landscape a joy to see? I started to sing. Presently I was standing in a brown doorway, looking into a wide, shabby kitchen, with a view of the hills, where a young woman in a flowered apron rolled pastry. Three kittens played at her feet, and a fair-haired little boy rocked himself wordlessly on a wooden horse. I explained my mission, swinging my basket as I spoke.

"Yes, I saw it in the paper. What a shame! Eating ponies! Barbaric, isn't it?"

She put down her rolling pin, brushed flour from her apron. "Toddlers' clothes always go well for jumble. Hang on, will you? I'll see what I can find. It's a damn shame, it really is." I watched the kittens, with the sun on my back, and made funny faces at the little boy, trying to make him laugh. The mother came back with some baby's rompers, a toddler's anorak, a pram rug and three *Ladybird* reading books.

"Won't you want the books for your son?" I asked.

"No, I've plenty more, not to worry," she said. "Here, I'll pop them in the basket for you. I wish you luck. We *all* wish you luck."

"Oh, wonderful! You are very kind," I said. "Thank you so much. We do appreciate your help."

I went on to a bungalow that stood behind firs, and then to a line of cottages on a ridge against the dark forest which stood on the outskirts of our little village, green and mysterious all the year through. By lunchtime I had as much jumble as I could carry. I staggered home to find Fergie sorting out a box of tools he had been given by a retired man who no longer needed them. The hall was now beginning to overflow with jumble so Mum gave us five cardboard boxes and told us to pack it up and put it in the barn.

We had just finished when a yellow Volvo drew up, from which stepped a smart woman in a quilted coat and brown trousers, with a large plastic bag under each arm.

"There, clothes in aid of those lovely ponies. Good luck! I think you're splendid!" she said. "Wait a minute, there's a bit more to come." She opened the hatch-back and out jumped a golden labrador. "No, not him," she said. "Here, lend me a hand, will you?" There was a pile of books, a typewriter, an old radio and a wind-up record player.

"Just junk, but someone will want it," she said. "They're lovely ponies—I could see from the photographs—some of them have a touch of Arab. Why *should* the French or Belgians eat them? Our government should put a stop to the trade. We're supposed to be a country of animal lovers, but I sometimes wonder."

We carried everything into the barn, thanking her effusively as we went.

"Oh, don't mention it," she replied. "We must thank *you* for your untiring efforts. I was so impressed that I packed all this lot up at once and drove ten miles. People like you should have a great deal of encouragement. After all, it's the young who have to make the world we oldsters will be living in soon."

By now the woman's labrador had chased our tabby cat, Tigger, up a tree, and was growling fiercely at our collie, Leerie. The next moment the two dogs had plunged into a battle. The labrador was the heavier, but although he dug his teeth into Leerie's throat he was quite unable to penetrate the fur, especially the soft sheep-like hair which lay between the outer layers of coat and skin.

24

We pulled the dogs apart eventually, and the woman in the green coat slapped and scolded the labrador.

"Wicked, evil animal. I *am* sorry," she said at last, pushing him into the car.

Later, our mother produced a large packet of pins and some scrap paper and we priced all the things for the jumble sale. It took ages and we argued a good deal, especially about how much we should charge for the typewriter. Fergie said fifteen pounds and I said twelve, so eventually Dad arbitrated and suggested thirteen pounds fifty, and we stuck to that.

The next day we rode up along Offa's Dyke to look at the ponies again. The dun, the bay and the smallest grey were lying down, looking like china ornaments. The others were standing nearby, each resting one hind leg.

"As if they've ever done anything to get tired," laughed Fergie. "I love that brown mare."

"Well, if we do buy them you must break her, then, and I bags the large grey. He's got the look of a leader about him."

"The jumble sale can't possibly yield six hundred pounds," said Fergie rather wearily. "I wonder whether we are being wildly optimistic."

"I think we could try Dad's bank manager," I said. "Surely he can see it's a fine financial proposition. Liz was right, we could call them after games, Jigsaw, Scrabble and so on."

"Now you're counting your chickens before they're hatched. For heaven's sake don't let us tempt providence," said my brother, who had a streak of pessimism as well as superstition.

"The skewbald is sweet," I said, refusing to be downcast. "Look at that lovely little face."

"Think of it being skinned," said Fergie. "Doesn't it make you sick? Sometimes I hate the human race."

We rode back rather gloomily. Our own ponies, Mimosa and Silverstar, were full of life and longing for a race.

25

They jogged and tossed their heads, but we wouldn't even let them canter.

"They must learn self-control," said Fergie sternly.

Mimosa's foal, Noodles, was waiting for us at the gate, his little chestnut face bright with welcome, his top lip twitching with excitement. And, when we dismounted, Tigger rubbed himself against our legs, purring loudly.

"We must clear the barn this afternoon. It's big enough for six, if we move most of the hay," said Fergie.

"But we may not get the ponies," I answered, thinking that it was my turn to be realistic. "And then all our efforts will be wasted!"

"We won't accept defeat until it actually arrives," said Fergie. "Something's *got* to happen."

"We need a patron," I said, and added on a spurt of inspiration, "We must go to the local master of foxhounds, to the District Commissioner of the Pony Club and to the Farmers' Union. Let's ring the R.S.P.C.A. on Monday."

"Yes," said Fergie, turning Silverstar out into the field. "But now I must go and write an essay on *For Whom The Bell Tolls*."

CHAPTER FOUR

A STROKE OF FATE

Saturday came all too quickly, and, as we set up the jumble sale in the village hall, we reminded ourselves that we had only until Monday to raise the six hundred pounds.

We had struggled during the week to borrow money, telephoning the R.S.P.C.A., whose secretary had said that her organisation could not possibly advance money to save ponies from the slaughterhouse. If they did, the lending would soon amount to many thousands of pounds, for the majority of livestock sold at sales such as those held at Reading and Stow-on-the-Wold were now exported for meat, some being transported alive, others being killed first. The R.S.P.C.A. at the moment, she said, was concentrating its efforts on improving transport conditions for all livestock being sent to the Continent.

The District Commissioner of the Pony Club expressed sympathy with our efforts, but said she could not lend Pony Club money without consulting the full committee which would not be meeting for another three weeks. She added that she would, however, be delighted to donate five pounds herself, which she sent by cheque the next day. The Farmers' Union was totally uninterested and the local master of foxhounds said we were making a damned fine effort, but he really couldn't use hunt funds to support us. My class at school kindly organised a cake sale which raised two pounds and five pence and a five pound note arrived anonymously through the post. That made a total of twelve pounds and five pence, so that at most we now hoped to save one pony, as our parents had promised to lend us money to make a total of one hundred pounds after we had totted up the financial rewards of the jumble sale.

We decided that the two taller ponies would eventually sell for the highest prices, but could not agree on which one to buy since Fergie favoured the dark brown and I the grey. Our parents told us we should have to toss up, and then I was disgusted by the thought that a toss of a coin should decide an issue of life and death.

As I smoothed the rompers and dusted the typewriter, I decided that I also hated the human race, most of whom put the importance of money above compassion. The ponies were, I reflected, far more beautiful than the men and women waiting to come in to buy our jumble.

Fergie looked at his watch. "Five minutes to go," he said.

"They look a fierce lot," remarked Trevor, one of two school friends who had come to help. "Some of those old women scare me. And look at the big bags they've brought."

"There's going to be a stampede," added Pippa, the other friend, who was tall, dark and beautiful with an elegance to which I could never aspire.

"Let's separate the children's books from the adult ones," I suggested. "Have they all been marked inside?" I started to look. "Isn't this a first edition?" I asked a moment later, turning the front pages of a novel.

"Give it to me," said Fergie, snatching. "Yes, for heaven's sake keep it. We must have that one valued."

"Two-thirty," called a plummy voice. "Time to open up."

"I'll go," offered Trevor, who is always obliging and level-headed.

We quickly arranged our tins of change and braced ourselves for the onslaught.

"At least they've *come*," said Pippa. "And you've been well supported. I mean you have a terrific lot of jumble."

"Some kind people brought boxes full to the hall this morning and our pony-trekking friend, Jake, managed to raise four sacks full," I explained.

And then our customers were upon us. The women all

pushed and shoved, snatching clothes from one another. The rompers were sold for eighty pence in a trice and the terrible collection of out-of-fashion hats soon went at ten pence each. A crowd of children pushed and shouted round the toys and books. We had arranged the tables in one long row with each of us looking after one. Pippa and I were in charge of clothes, while Fergie and Trevor sold the other things. There was one enormous woman who kept asking me about the size of things while her companion quietly shoved other items into her own bag without paying. We spotted the thief just in time and Trevor, who had ambitions to be a Chief Constable, went after her and insisted that she came back and emptied her bag, but, while she did so, someone else must have stolen the radio because soon afterwards we found it missing. The thieving woman was unrepentant. It was up to us to keep an eye on things, she said, angrily throwing the stolen goods back on the table, while the enormous woman who was obviously her collaborator said jumble sales were always a bit of a free-for-all. You paid for some things and nicked the rest. That was normal practice. A lot of the stuff was little better than rubbish anyway. And we couldn't argue, because now we realised we must watch everyone all the time and there was no time to talk. As the pile of money in the tins grew, we stuffed the notes into our pockets for safety. Then, mercifully, our parents arrived to see how we were getting on.

"They're shoplifting," I said simply. "We've lost the radio already and Fergie only just managed to stop someone nicking the typewriter."

"All right. Carry on. I'll be the security officer," said Dad, who was not easily intimidated.

"I'll look after the money, empty the tins and check on change," hissed Mum.

With grown-ups in view, the attitude of the customers seemed to become more respectful. They counted the money more carefully into our palms and pushed less. A little man with a Charlie Chaplin moustache bought the

29

typewriter and a lank youth, with an outsize adam's apple, the record player. The books went more slowly; the children, with little money to spend, seemed more interested in toys and games. The tools went to a sun-tanned manual worker who returned home to get the necessary cash from his wife, who, he said wryly, held the purse strings.

"I'll have to get her permission, mind," he said, with a broad smile.

At last satisfied, the women with the big bags and loose coats left in a crowd.

"You'll be better without them. They come to every darned sale. Got a lift from Craven Arms, I shouldn't wonder. It's like a profession to them—the more they can pinch the better they are pleased," said a little woman with a wrinkled face and greying hair stretched back into a bun.

"Predators they are, like a lot of crows after a corpse. 'Orrible!" put in the man who had come back with the money for the tools. "They don't care for charity nor nothing."

"We could do with some of those books for our old people's home. It's desperately short of reading matter. But only highly respectable stuff, nothing too modern or way-out," said a sprightly, bird-like little woman, eyes sparkling with merriment. "I do hope you've made lots of money. After all, if you only save one pony, that is still something."

I collected books for her and tied them with string. Then suddenly the sale was over, the place was empty except for us. Our mother had been counting the money.

"Hand in the last bits and pieces, please," she said.

There seemed a lot of pound notes but we knew we couldn't possibly have made more than fifty or so.

"I hated some of our customers," I said.

"You're not the only one," added Trevor. "People say teenagers are rude, but I don't know a single person in my age group who would push and cheat like that batch."

"Sixty pounds, twenty-seven and one half pence," said Mum. "Congratulations!"

"If the radio hadn't been pinched the sum would have been over seventy pounds," said Fergie bitterly.

"Oh, don't take it to heart, jumble sales are always a fiasco," said Dad. "Now we must tidy up. Put all the unsold things into cardboard boxes. You've done very well."

As he spoke, the door opened and a thick-set man, wearing a woolly cap, came in.

"I saw about the sale in the paper," he explained. "I deal in old clothes and buy up anything that's left, especially the wool. I'll give you a fair price."

"Well, look here, there's quite a pile," I said.

He turned it over with thick, work-worn hands. He had a scar running down one side of his face, curly brown hair, and small, sunken, blue eyes.

"I'll give you a pound for the lot," he said.

"Fair enough," said Dad.

"We'll accept that, won't we?" Fergie asked me, glancing reproachfully at our father for interfering.

The man handed over a grubby note.

"Can I take a box I've got the van outside."

"Of course," we said. "We'll help."

"Hand us a coin, Mum," said Fergie when the man had gone. "We must toss up to decide which pony to save."

"I'll do it," offered Dad, digging in his pocket. "Heads or tails, Sandy, and if you win you choose."

"Tails," I cried, seeing in my mind's eye that graceful darkish grey with the head of an Arab and the wonderful sturdiness of a Welsh pony who has grown on the hills.

Dad tossed; the silver fivepence spun in the air and fell to be caught in the palm of his hand.

"Sorry, heads," he said. "Your choice, Fergie."

"The brown mare. Sorry, Sandy," said my brother.

It was all over. We had lost the campaign. I thought of the humane killer, the smell of blood in the abattoir which would frighten the grey as he dashed out of the cattle truck, shaking with fear and apprehension, his large eyes

31

bulging with terror, his nostrils dilated. There had been too little time.

"Jake says Mr. Jones promised they would be killed nearby. They won't make a terrible journey to the Continent," said my mother, touching me.

We started to pack the remaining books into a box.

"This one is a first edition, Dad," said Fergie. "So we put it to one side."

"1930. Good. It'll fetch a pound or two I expect, but not a fortune—now if it had been Sir Walter Scott or Dickens . . ." mused our father.

"I'll ring up old George for advice," offered Mum. "His second wife's first husband is in the trade, so we shan't be cheated."

I didn't care. It was too late, anyway. I thought the talk a waste of time. I wanted to pick up the book and throw it across the floor, to say what did a first edition matter when the other five ponies were to be destroyed, to be eaten by humans, baked in ovens, grilled, stewed, munched up by greedy foreigners?

I picked up a few unsold toys and tossed them on top of the books. Tears were pricking at the back of my eyes, and a ridiculous lump had lodged itself in my throat. I didn't want to speak to anyone. I wanted to run away and bury my face in the damp September earth and cry. We had been beaten before we had really begun.

"It's not as though you haven't got three lovely ponies already," said Dad.

"It's not that," I shouted. "I don't want them for *myself*. Don't you understand? They're beautiful and full of life and joy and . . ." I stopped and turned away because I felt the tears coming and I didn't want Trevor and Pippa to see my crying.

"You're being tactless, James," said my mother.

And then we all fell silent, for there was a little old woman with a stick walking across the hall, a funny little hat on the top of her head and an old wise smile on her face.

"I'm very sorry, but the sale has finished," said Fergie, stepping forward with a polite little bow.

"Ah, you would be Fergus Hamilton, then? Am I right?" The old lady had a rusty little voice which was not without charm. She peered into his face with short-sighted blue eyes.

"Oh, yes, indeed," said Fergie, taken aback.

"And which is Sandy then?"

"Me, here." I held out my hand after brushing away the tears.

"I read about it in the paper. Such a shame! I learned to ride on a little Welsh pony myself—many years ago, of course. We called her Starlight. Bright as a button she was, but so gentle."

The old lady smiled as though her mind was going back and back to happier days when the sun always shone and the world was a kind and wonderful place. She had a very small, delicate face with a sharp little nose and yet the air of one who had once been accustomed to commanding others, and she was upright and in no way pathetic.

"I'm Mrs. Wellbeloved, and your father was very kind to my sister-in-law when we had illness in the family," she explained. "He drove her to the hospital in his taxi and nothing was too much trouble for him. You must be a wonderful family."

"Oh, no, not at all," replied Fergie, while our parents retreated into the background. "We just love animals."

"And so do I. I think in many respects they could teach us humans a lesson, but we're too arrogant to see that, far too arrogant. Well now, I mustn't beat about the bush. You must be wondering why I've come."

"A little bit," said Fergie, with a very pleasant, encouraging smile.

"Well," she said again, "I have a little inheritance which has just come in, which I was going to put in a Building Society for the time being, but seeing the paper last Saturday I began to wonder whether I could loan it to you instead? It's only five hundred pounds, but I think that

33

will cover your immediate needs, and it would give me great pleasure to keep the dear ponies off the foreigners' dinner tables."

She paused, and seeing that we were speechless, went on. "I've spoken with my lawyer and he will draw up a document. I shall not want any interest. You can keep any profit you make for yourselves. It seemed so extraordinary, like a stroke of fate, you see, with the cheque arriving on my breakfast table along with the paper and your photograph. I don't think it was a coincidence. Some things are *meant*. It was a message from on high."

"I don't know what to say," began Fergie. "We're so tremendously grateful. We thought we had failed and now suddenly . . ."

"Well, don't be grateful," said the old lady promptly, tapping the floor with her stick. "I'm only helping you to do a wonderful thing. I'm pleased to help. We must all be grateful to young people like you who *care*. Caring is so important, you see. It's what is missing so often today."

I thought of the grey in our barn, of the little dun and the pretty skewbald, and the bay with the ridiculous and endearing blaze like a splash of milk on his face, and, taking a big gulp, I said: "But, you've made this one of the best days of our lives. You're a fairy godmother. You've actually saved the ponies. We could only afford one until you walked into this hall and now we can afford all six. I can't believe it. It feels like a dream."

"You will, you will," said the old lady. "Now, who shall I write the cheque to?"

"Oh, we've already opened a special account called The Pony Fund," said Fergie.

"I shall instruct my lawyer and the cheque and document will be with you first thing Tuesday morning," smiled Mrs. Wellbeloved.

And Fergie said, "I think you ought to meet our parents —and these are our kind helpers, Trevor and Pippa."

I sat down on a bench because suddenly my legs felt as though they were made of cotton wool.

CHAPTER FIVE

SOME PEOPLE HAVE ALL THE LUCK

We went up to the field the next day and looked again at the ponies, hardly believing that a dream was about to come true.

"Shall we have three each?" suggested Fergie.

"All right." I glanced at the grey, standing alone, eyeing us. "Which would be your second choice, following the brown?"

"Well," said Fergie after a long pause, "I suppose the dun, not because he's the prettiest, but because my legs are longer than yours and he's a little taller than the rest."

"All right, I'll take the skewbald," I said. "She's the smallest. And the bay with the white blaze, and that leaves you a grey, to brighten your less brilliant colours. After all, if I have *two* greys I shall be for ever washing tails."

"That's settled then. What about names?" asked Fergie.

I reminded him then that we hadn't received Mrs. Wellbeloved's cheque yet and, as Dad said, we might find something impossible to sign in the document. "She may be a crank," I finished, turning away, unable to face the possibility that our dream might be shattered.

"Yes, I suppose it *could* be too good to be true. I mean fairy godmothers are simply fantasy. They don't really exist," agreed my brother.

We mounted our ponies again. Today I was riding Silverstar, who was 14.2, and Fergie rode Mimosa.

After crossing into England again, we cantered back along the Dyke. Silverstar was well-schooled with a long effortless stride. She bent her head to the bit and dropped her lower jaw and was wonderfully supple. Mimosa was more of a dumpling with a shorter stride, but merry and

35

enjoyable just the same, with a bouncy canter. She was a cheerful, willing hack, interested in everything, once she had accepted that her rider was in charge, but she was less enjoyable to ride in the school, as she lacked Silverstar's cadence and suppleness. Anyone knowing a bit about conformation could see that she wasn't made for more than the most elementary dressage; her neck was a little too thick where it joined her head; her action was rather high; and she hadn't the lightness and elegance necessary for a dressage horse. She was our first pony. Noodles was her son, an unexpected bonus for we didn't know she was in foal when we bought her.

When we were home again our mother pointed out that we would need headcollars and some extra tack, and so we began to feel weighed down again by the need to raise money. Then we remembered that, with the trekking season just ended, Jake might have a few halters to spare, so we rode up to his place, where a group of bantams scratched happily in the morning sunshine.

He was out in the yard, tinkering with the engine of one of his cattle trucks.

"Hullo there. How do?" He turned round, small, very wiry with a lean, expressive face, his hands black with oil. "What's up now?"

"Nothing," answered Fergie grinning. "Only we thought you might like to know that an old lady has promised to loan us five hundred pounds."

"Never!" said Jake.

"Oh yes," we cried, and then in a rush, interrupting each other, we explained.

"Well, some people have all the luck! No one's ever come to my rescue with five hundred pounds," said Jake, rubbing his hands on a rag. "So now you're all set up."

"Well, we must wait to see whether there are any snags in the lawyer's document. We don't think there will be because she genuinely wanted to help," said Fergie.

"If there are they'll soon be smoothed out. We've already written to Emlyn Jones, and Dad's delivering the letter by hand, because he's got a job that way this morning," I explained, feeling optimistic again.

"Well done! My congratulations then," said Jake with a wry grin before turning back to his lorry.

"We're wondering," I began. "I mean, now your ponies are going to their winter homes . . ."

"Yes?" said Jake, his head coming up with a jerk. "What's it this time?"

"Halters, headcollars? Do they go with your ponies when you farm them out for the winter?"

"Not always," said Jake. "I reckon I could find you half a dozen, and a lunge reign and whip."

"You're an angel," I said.

"No, I don't want to start growing wings, not yet awhile. The good Lord must be content with other messengers to do his work," replied Jake, with a grin. "Go up to the caravan and help yourselves. You're welcome." He threw us a key and then turned back to his engine.

"Problem one settled," I announced, turning Silverstar in a pirouette. And Fergie said: "A thousand thanks."

The document was straightforward. It made our parents guarantors for the loan, which was for eight weeks, and a letter from the solicitor suggested that we insured the ponies for five hundred pounds. We signed it before we went to school, and Dad said he would pay in the cheque for us that morning, and see a man he knew connected with a leading insurance company. "It shouldn't cost much, as the policy has only to cover a short time," he said.

"We might take longer to find them good homes," I put in.

"Well, initially, anyway," he said. "You should be able to part with two or three of them at six weeks, if you work hard, and if I can run the electricity out to the barn and stockyard."

"The trouble is the evenings will be getting dark so soon

and school takes up too much time," I complained. "We can't do everything in a yard."

"Never trouble trouble till trouble troubles you," quoted Dad maddeningly.

In the evening we wrote out a cheque for six hundred pounds to Mr. Emlyn Jones, and my hand trembled for I had never signed a cheque before and the sum seemed truly enormous.

Jake came down to talk about transport.

"I've been thinking," he said. "It's only five miles, and the lanes are narrow and well-protected with hedges. Why don't we drive the ponies down? My old collie bitch will lend a hand. We can have two of us behind and one in front. I've got a couple of hunting whips. There are no real roads until the last half mile to your house and your parents can lend a hand there."

"So long as the ponies don't get killed by a car," I said.

"But this time of year there are only farmers and their like up in the lanes," said Jake. "And there's only one little crossroads. and your Dad can be there to help out."

And so it was that by Wednesday evening, just before dark, the ponies were safely esconced in our yard, looking very wild and startled, with Leerie lying by the fence, keeping an eye on them.

"Ping Pong," said Fergie.

"Ping pong what?"

"I'm naming the little grey Ping Pong—you know, table tennis."

"Oh, all right, so long as it's never shortened to Pong," I said. "She looks bouncy enough."

"Exactly."

"And Hopscotch for my little dun," he added.

"That's quick work," I said.

"I was thinking as we drove them down that lane, but the brown must wait. She's special. I must study her character."

"No favouritism," I said.

"Jigsaw for the little bay," suggested Jake. "That white

marking down his face has the jagged look of a jigsaw piece."

"Is jigsaw a game?" asked my brother.

"Of course," I said. "Thanks, Jake."

"What about the grey. How about Scrabble?"

"He doesn't look a scrabbly sort of person."

"You're mixing it up with scramble," complained my brother. "People who win scrabble are serious—good spellers. He looks serious. Watch him now. He's apart from the others, thinking. He's an individualist."

"I shall call him Solitaire, then," I shouted, on a wave of inspiration.

"That suits him down to the ground," said my mother.

"And the skewbald needs further thought."

"The next owners will change their names, anyway," said my brother. "So there's no point in taking the matter too seriously."

"Well, I'll be off now," said Jake. "I'm glad we got them down safe and sound. It's a lot better than driving them all into one of those trucks and frightening them out of their wits."

"Sure you won't have a glass of something?" asked Dad. But Jake said, "No, thanks all the same," and the next moment he was jogging away up the road on his liver chestnut Bournville.

"He's a real card, but a brick, too," said Dad. "You can't help liking the man."

CHAPTER SIX

WE'VE SO LITTLE TIME

Our comprehensive school finished at three-fifteen, with only those belonging to clubs or wishing to use the library or classrooms for homework staying on. We usually reached home at four o'clock, but rather earlier if we ran from the bus stop. On the Thursday after the ponies' arrival we were in the yard by three-fifty-five, sitting amongst them offering handfuls of grass. They were all fat, and we had given them only a little hay in the morning so that they would be hungry and ready to approach us in the evening. Fergie called that *commonsense training*.

"We are the good friends who relieve them of their hunger," he said. "Here, Ping Pong, come on! I won't hurt you."

The little grey and Jigsaw looked at us curiously from under long dark lashes, their eyes peering through forelocks of hair.

"If we stay very still, they'll come and sniff us eventually," added my brother.

But it was the skewbald who came first, very cautiously approaching me as I sat with my back against the fence, one hand holding out grass. I thought she was coming just for the grass, but she stopped and tentatively sniffed my feet before grabbing it, and then jumping back quickly as though I might spring up like a jack-in-the-box and strike her. Hopscotch, the dun, stretched out his neck and took some of the grass from the skewbald's mouth.

"That's hardly fair," said Fergie, and at the sound of his voice, all the ponies dashed back into the barn.

"We must talk a lot so that our voices become part of

everyday life for them, as expected as the birds' songs," I said.

It was a slow business, but, after an hour, three ponies; the skewbald, Jigsaw and Hopscotch had all summoned the courage to take grass from our hands. The other three preferred to remain hungry. Ping Pong seemed excessively nervous and the brown and Solitaire too proud to make friends with those who had robbed them of their freedom.

After tea, in the dusk, we led Noodles, our yearling. up and down so that the wild ponies could see how civilised young ponies behaved. We fed him grass in front of them, and eventually Solitaire came forward to take a mouthful before retreating rapidly.

Later, Dad worked by the light of a hurricane lantern to extend the electrical circuit so that we could light the barn and yard and train the ponies after dark, talking to them as he fixed the cable and junction boxes, while they watched him as though he were some extraordinary person from Mars, their eyes very large and their ears pricked.

The next morning we rose at half-past six, and, taking the lantern, we went back to the yard and fed our hungry captives with handfuls of grass again. This time the skewbald, Jigsaw and Hopscotch came to us without hesitation, their stomachs rumbling, and the brown mare and Solitaire more cautiously. Little Ping Pong remained aloof. In the evening, Jigsaw welcomed us with a little whinny and we were able to stroke his neck.

The next day was Saturday and the ponies whom we had fed with the minimum amount of hay were beginning to look tucked-up and were obviously very hungry. We took it in turns to spend the morning with them and, by lunchtime, they had eaten carrots, sliced lengthwise, grass, hay and a few oats, from our hands, and we had been able to stroke their necks. Only Ping Pong remained frightened of us. The others were cautious but friendly, and at midday we were able to slip headcollars on to the skewbald and Hopscotch. Mother managed to find a packet of cube sugar in her store cupboard and that proved to be the downfall of Ping Pong, for once she had tasted and eaten one cube she could not resist begging for more, although she was still too quick and nervous to allow us to touch the back of her head. But, now knowing her greed for sugar, we felt it would not be long before she gave in.

In the afternoon we schooled Mimosa and Silverstar in the field which could be seen from the barn and yard so that our captives could watch, for we wanted them to consider it quite normal to be ridden when the time came for us to back them. Later, we spent another three hours in the yard, so that the ponies began to think of us as one of them. We ate slices of lardy cake and drank tea, sitting amongst them on the damp earth, and after a few minutes Solitaire came across and sniffed my hair, and then Ping Pong, hungry for sugar, upset Fergie's tea.

By nightfall they were all wearing headcollars and we could run our hands along their necks and shoulders. We refilled their water trough and gave them six large piles of hay and went indoors to do our homework. Dad finished the lighting arrangement, and, before going to bed, we took the ponies cubes of sugar. Jigsaw, Solitaire and Hopscotch all welcomed us with a whinny; and we held each of them in turn by the headcollar as the sugar was eaten.

The next morning we took them sliced apples. The skewbald came up first, her eyes bright with anticipation. She was the smallest of all, and I decided then on the spur of the moment to call her Tiddly-Winks.

"She really is rather tiddly and I'm sure she's full of spring," I said somewhat banally.

"The brown always waits till last, so I'm going to call her Patience," announced Fergie, as though not to be outdone. "I thought of it in bed last night. Do you remember how Mr. Duckworth, our neighbour in Sonnywood, used to play patience in the evenings to settle his nerves?"

I didn't, but I thought the name a good one for the mare, who did indeed have a look of patience, almost of resignation, about her.

Once again, we spent most of the day with our new friends. We clipped ropes to the headcollars of Patience, Solitaire, Hopscotch and Tiddly-Winks and led them up and down, as we had led Noodles in front of them two days earlier, and they seemed to accept our behaviour as normal and did not pull back or try to rush forward. We let them grow accustomed to the idea that our pockets were full of tasty tit-bits, and they began to nuzzle us as soon as we came into the yard. We gave them plenty of hay and they soon lost their tucked-up look. Solitaire continued to find my hair interesting. I think he thought it should be edible as it was the colour of straw and smelt perpetually of the hay I was always carting about. Tiddly-Winks took a special interest in my feet and, after a bit, chewed one of my shoe laces in half, while Jigsaw sucked a sleeve of my jersey, as though sampling its taste.

Soon Fergie was running his hands down Patience's legs and I was leaning across Tiddly-Winks' back. I thought I would ride her first, because, if things went wrong, I would not have far to fall.

"Mind you," said Jake, who came down that evening to see how we were getting on, "the little 'uns are often the craftiest. But if you take them all slowly there shouldn't be any trouble. If they buck, that means you've taken them too fast. Once they trust you they won't mind you on their backs. Why should they?"

"We've so little time, five days have gone already," complained Fergie.

"But the groundwork always takes a long time. Once you've got that right, you can make strides. I think you've done wonders taming them so fast. I couldn't have done better myself, and this little fenced yard is just the job," said our friend. "But if you have any worries, come and see me. I shall be pleased to do anything I can."

"You've done so much already. We are completely indebted to you," I said.

"Ah, but I've got a lot to repay, haven't I? What about that time I broke my leg and you managed the whole

43

trek?* I should have lost pounds and a good deal of future custom but for you," said Jake. "The shoe's not just on one foot. It's a two-way thing."

"Which do you like best?" I asked, embarrassed by gratitude.

"What, which of those ponies? I couldn't say that, could I, seeing you've shared them out? Why, I should offend one of you and I wouldn't want to do that." Jake gave his wry grin. "They're a fine lot and no mistake. That skewbald will make a wonderful leading-rein pony, should win some classes I shouldn't wonder, and the brown mare's got a wise look about her which catches my fancy. They're all hard to fault, aren't they? P'raps the dun isn't such a good-looker as the rest, but then duns are always wonderfully hardy and he'll make a good, reliable first pony—bomb-proof, I'd say, and that's what parents want these days, isn't it? Something that'll stand up to any amount of traffic and noise."

"I think I like Solitaire best," I said.

"The tall grey? He's got breeding about him, but don't you think his feet turn in a fraction in front? He's just a little bit pigeon-toed to my way of thinking, but a fine pony, mind you, with the best shoulder of the lot."

"The brown mare," put in Fergie quickly. "I reckon she's the best, look at that length of neck, and how well her pasterns slope. There's a great look of breeding about Patience."

"Yes, she's a grand mare," agreed Jake, lighting a cigarette. "No mistake there, she's hard to fault, but she hasn't quite the bone of that little Jigsaw, has she? Why, that little blighter would carry a man and keep going all day."

"Bone?" said Fergie.

"Well, look," said Jake. "She's a bit delicate, isn't she? See, her cannon bones aren't quite as wide as Solitaire's. She's a lovely mare, mind you, but not quite as strong as some of the others, not up to weight."

* *Ponies on the Trail.*

44

"Well, they're not meant to be show horses," said Fergie, slightly affronted.

"But they'd all do you credit in a ring. Don't get me wrong, Fergie, I'm being as critical as I can, and you can't expect to get champions at a hundred pounds apiece now, can you? It doesn't make blooming sense. Mind you, the skewbald could be a winner."

As we inspected our ponies with pride, Mummy called us into supper, and Jake said he must be on his way for a game of darts at the pub.

"They're a bit short just now and they want me in the team," he explained. "I expect they'll regret that decision, but there's no changing their minds!"

CHAPTER SEVEN

THE FIRST SETBACK

The next week we started to lunge the ponies, beginning on a very short rein, making a triangle out of rein, whip and animal with ourselves at the apex. With sugar in our pockets we soon taught them to stop at "whoa" and turn in, when told, to be suitably rewarded. The greediest, Hopscotch, Jigsaw and Tiddly-Winks, watched us closely as they walked, waiting for the invitation, at which they would swing round and dash in with ill-disguised anticipation. Tiddly-Winks actually licking her lips as she came. Ping Pong, however, was too highly-strung, and Solitaire and Patience too dignified and thoughtful to follow the others' example.

Although it was now the end of September, we were blessed with clear weather and cloudless skies which made the evenings wonderfully light. The nights were silver as the moon sailed in the heavens, and owls called from barn and tree. All our actions in the yard were closely watched by Leerie, who guarded our captives until we called him in last thing at night before Dad locked up. Tigger, who was supposed to sleep out, soon started spending his nights on Hopscotch's broad, plump back, purring gently. In general, our six ponies seemed to be settling down well, and we were pleased when some of them welcomed us with a whinny in the mornings when we brought them hay and checked their water before going to school.

Now we taught them to stand still while being groomed, to pick up their hooves when asked and move over when we touched them on either flank. Gradually they all learned to walk and trot on the lunge rein to the appropriate commands. The yard was too small for cantering and soon became too dirty and wet to be entirely satisfactory. We cleaned the barn, which was bedded down in straw, daily, and picked droppings from the yard, which had only an earth base until Dad bought a load of peat, which we spread out so that for a time there was a good surface for lunging. Later, Dad said, he would sell it along with the manure to a local market-gardener.

By Wednesday, Solitaire, Patience, Jigsaw and Hopscotch had all worn saddles, and by Thursday, Ping Pong and Tiddly-Winks had been bridled. We had no mouthing bits, just a couple of jointed snaffles which they sucked and jingled in their mouths.

Our chief adviser was Jake, who had had much experience of breaking-in ponies. He wasn't a very accomplished rider and knew little about dressage, as he was the first to admit, but he was very good at handling animals. He could make the wildest quiet in a few days and not one of his ponies kicked, bit or showed any fear of humans. They were all co-operative and sweet-tempered. In addition, we possessed a book on training horses, which we found invaluable, as it went into great detail about such matters as "approaching a pony with a saddle for the first time" and "your first visit to the blacksmith".

Yet, although things were going well, Fergie was obsessed with the feeling that time was running out and we would not have the ponies ready to sell within six or eight weeks.

"We still have to train them in traffic and hack them alone and in company," he wailed one evening, as he saddled Ping Pong. "And we haven't even sat on their backs yet. Whoa, stand!" The little grey eyed him nervously. She hated the feel of the girth being pulled up. "Right, now, walk on!" She was tense, as stiff as someone in the dentist's chair waiting for the drill. She didn't like the saddle; she felt squeezed between its cold leather and the tautness of the nylon girth.

"Walk on," repeated Fergie.

"I'll lead her," I offered, but I was too late, for the

next moment she had plunged forward, the lunge rein had slipped through Fergie's hand and she was hurling herself at the yard fence; the wood cracked, then splintered and, in an instant, she was outside, going down the drive to the road, bucking and plunging like a wild west bronco, desperate to rid herself of the unknown monster on her back.

Leerie ran after her, barking wildly, trying to get in front to head her off, but Ping Pong was too fast for him.

"Oh, God, don't let there be a car," I prayed. "Nor a lorry nor a truck nor any blessed thing!"

"Keep the others back while I go," yelled Fergie, leaping over the fence. "Mend the fence or something. Don't just stand there gaping!"

Hopscotch, who was Ping Pong's special friend, neighed as I started to try to pull together the broken pieces of wood. They wouldn't meet and soon I fetched a pole and tied it across the gap with baling string. Then I slipped a bridle on Mimosa, who had been watching over the hedge, and set off down the road in pursuit of Ping Pong, Leerie and my brother.

Dusk was falling. The fine weather was over. On either side the hills stood absolutely still as though waiting for night to draw across the black curtains of darkness. The sky was mainly grey with streaks of yellow where the last rays of the sun splintered the west, and a blackbird was singing in a pollarded willow that stood, hunched as an old man, by the river. Cows, suspecting rain, were beginning to lie down to secure warm dry patches for the night.

"Saw a little grey pony go by. Wild she was, terrified. She won't stop this side of Clun," said an elderly man wheeling a bicycle.

"And a dog and a boy?"

"The pony ten minutes back," he said. "Them just after."

Coming to a grass verge, I cantered Mimosa, my mind full of awful forebodings. Then ahead of me I saw a cattle truck parked across the road.

"Jake!"

But it wasn't our friend. A stranger with a fair, clean-shaven face and southern accent stood in the road. Fergie was there, too, with Leerie and, most important of all, little Ping Pong, drooping like a punctured ball.

"Everything all right?" I called, bringing Mimosa to a trot as the verge merged into the road.

"No," called back my brother. "She's damaged."

"I put the truck across the road to stop her, like, and she was that mad she crashed right into it," said the driver.

"Lots of cuts," said Fergie. "We'll have to get a vet." His face looked white and strained as he turned from the pony to welcome me with a sort of forced smile.

The elderly man caught up, riding his bicycle, which looked at least twenty years old.

"You caught her then?"

"She's bleeding from three legs and her chest. She'll have to be stitched."

Fergie was examining the last of the wounds.

" 'Ang on," said the man with the bike, dismounting. "I've an old-fashioned remedy, used to use it before the First World War. My Dad was a carter. 'E knew about 'orses. 'Ad a team once."

"I never thought she'd crash into the truck, I only meant to stop her," the driver said again, his brow creased with anxiety and remorse. "It's a damn shame. She's a pretty little pony."

"She's suffering from shock," said Fergie, applying pressure just below a wound on her shoulder, which was bleeding freely. "I don't think she's cut an artery, but maybe a vein."

The little pony was shivering, so I gave her sugar from my pocket. Leerie was sitting on the side of the road looking ashamed of himself.

The elderly man came back with a triumphant smile on his face which knocked off ten years of old age. "See," he said. "In that old shed." He seemed to have rags in his hands, nylon or something.

49

"I hope they're clean, otherwise they'll infect the wound," I began.

"Them not clean," he replied firmly. "But there'll be no more bleeding when I've done. I've watched my father many a time. Wonderful man, my father. Knew all the old remedies, none of this new-fangled stuff."

He leaned down, his faded blue eyes peering from under his cap at Ping Pong's knee. "There," he said gently, covering the wound. "Now the shoulder."

"Cobwebs!" cried Fergie, astounded.

"Ah, I've heard tell of them, for wounds," said the young truck driver. "But I've never seen it done before."

"And you probably won't ever see it done again, 'cos the young don't 'old with such things, it's all penicillin these days, but that's only mould isn't it? And my old Dad always said mould from off an old bun was a wonderful thing to clear up infection."

"It's stopped the bleeding," said Fergie in wonderment. "It really has."

The old man was cryptic: "Well, don't you go killing any more spiders, then. It's not only King Bruce who's found 'em useful."

"I never do, actually," replied Fergie. "Nor does Sandy."

"Well, that's the last wound," said the man, with great satisfaction. "All dressed now till you can get your 'orse doctor along with his modern medicine."

"You're wonderful," I said. "Do tell us your name."

"I don't want any reward, none of that sort of thing. It's been a pleasure." The man straightened his back. "When you get old it does you a power of good to be useful now and then."

"We would like to bring the pony to see you when she's better, or something," I said.

"I'll tell you what then," said our new friend, taking off his cap to scratch his head of white hair. "You can let me have a sack of manure for my garden, that would be very welcome."

"Right," said Fergie. "Oh, look at that!"

We had been so wrapped up in Ping Pong that we had quite forgotten that we were blocking the road, and now, turning round, we saw that a line of cars stretched beyond the truck, and one moustached man was bearing down on us, his gooseberry green eyes bulging with aggression.

"I'm supposed to be at St. David's before nightfall," he exploded. "What the devil do you think you're doing?"

"Tell me your address quickly. I shall remember," I whispered to the man with the bicycle, while the truck driver ran to his cab and started the engine with a great roar.

"There's been an accident. The pony was nearly killed. I'm sorry, we'll move now," said Fergie equably, starting to lead the limping Ping Pong away towards home. Then he turned. "Her saddle's in the hedge, can you bring it, please, Sandy?" While I put it on Mimosa, the truck went slowly by and I called out my thanks to the driver.

"Hope she heals all right," he said.

The other cars came past us, the moustached man looking furious because he was stuck behind an old lady driving a Mini who was obviously going to crawl along at twenty miles an hour for ages.

At our request, a vet came later that evening, injected Ping Pong against tetanus and stitched two of the wounds. Young and fresh-faced, he was amazed at the cobwebs and our explanation. "I've heard some old wives' tales in my time, but that takes the ticket," he said, gently bathing away the cobwebs before applying penicillin ointment.

"Still, it works. It makes the blod clot," argued Fergie.

"Yes, I can see that," the young vet said. "I read about you in the paper. I wish you luck, by the way. But I shall have to charge you I'm afraid."

"Yes, of course," I said. "We didn't expect otherwise."

"It's our first setback," said my brother. "I suppose she'll be scarred for life."

"Well, things can't go smoothly *all* the time," said the vet, shutting his case. "There you are, my sweet, keep calm next time." He patted Ping Pong. "She's a great little pony. Shouldn't be hard to sell her once she's settled."

CHAPTER EIGHT

WE'RE REALLY MAKING PROGRESS

"I'm afraid we may have spoiled her for ever," said Fergie, sitting on a bale of straw, chewing a strand of hay. "I mean, I daren't lunge her again in a saddle, so how shall I get her used to it? I feel I'm in a vicious circle."

"No, no, not at all," said Jake cheerfully. "Don't lunge her in a saddle again. If I were you I should sit on her bareback the first time."

"But we can't sell a pony that can't be ridden in proper tack," argued Fergie, his face pessimistic.

"I didn't say that, did I?" replied Jake. "You see, when there's no weight in the saddle there's much more pressure on the belly if you pull the girth tight, and some horses don't like that. But the minute you sit in the saddle the pressure goes, so often it's wisest not to tighten up until you've mounted. Little Ping Pong felt trapped, squeezed between saddle and girth. Did you let her have a good sniff at everything first?"

"Well, yes," began my brother a little doubtfully.

"And the *well* means not as long as you should have done. I can read you like a book, Fergie. No, you pulled them girths too tight too quickly, and you never let her have a good old sniff round the saddle. You must start again with that particular operation much later on. Leave the saddle aside for a bit."

"But the book . . ."

"Never mind the book. The author couldn't go into every possible difficulty. Now, what about the rest? How are the other ponies getting on?"

"We're backing them today," I said.

"Not all, I hope," said Jake. "They can't all be ready

at the same time. Ponies are individuals. They're like children. They need to go at different speeds."

"Well, the quietest," I said.

"Have you had your Dad driving the bus by the yard yet?"

I said no, and Jake said we should ask him right away, as we must accustom the ponies to traffic as soon as possible, before we went on the road. Saturday was as good a day as any, and he reckoned that within the next week we might easily ride a couple of the ponies up to see him.

"You're their friends now. They won't mind you on their backs," he said. "But get them used to cars first."

Two weeks had passed since the jumble sale and nine days since the ponies' arrival on the farm.

"It's a race against time," said Fergie as we rode down the lane to home. "Only thirty-three more days and then we should think of selling."

"The little ones first," I said, "because although we are so light, we look a bit long-legged and ridiculous on them. Hopscotch and Jigsaw will soon be ready."

"Will they?" asked my brother. "Remember, the little ones must be sold to little people, which means they must be dead quiet."

"Well then, we shall have to sell Patience and Solitaire first, which will be a wrench, but will cut the size of the loan considerably," I replied, trying to be practical.

That day we started to lead the ponies round the fields, each in turn, with one of us holding the lunge rein and the other a rope clipped to their headcollars.

"A bit unprofessional, perhaps," said Fergie, "but a double insurance policy. We can't have any more galloping away up the road."

Hopscotch and Tiddly-Winks, who were both four, went quietly, but Jigsaw, who was five, was nervous and inclined to snort and shy at birds moving in the hedges. After lunch we tacked up Mimosa and Silverstar, mounted, and led Patience and Solitaire from them, being careful to keep the field gate shut. Having learned the words of com-

53

mand on the lunge rein, our pupils readily obeyed the order to trot on and kept up well with our mounts. In this way we exercised them for half an hour, taking the edge off their energy. Then Fergie saddled Patience in the yard where the ground was soft, and, while I stood at her head, murmuring soft endearments, he put a foot in the left stirrup and practised jumping up and down. The brown mare barely moved and seemed quite unconcerned, so, after a while, he lay across the saddle, patting her shoulder on the off side. Then very gently, talking all the time, he slipped on her back and sat in the saddle. Her ears flickered, her eyes moved back a fraction in their sockets, but there were no danger signals; she didn't stiffen or show the slightest fear.

"Patience," Fergie leaned down a fraction and, knowing that that particular tone of voice usually meant sugar, the brown mare brought her head round and a moment later was actually munching a cube between her molars.

"Good," said Fergie, sliding off again. "Shall I repeat it?"

"Yes, why not? Then you must hold Solitaire."

The next try was successful, too, and with another cube of sugar in her mouth, Patience looked genuinely pleased to be mounted, like a young child who has just performed a feat usually restricted to grown-ups. Meanwhile, the taller grey had been watching with pricked ears and was prepared for his turn, thinking no doubt of the sugar he might soon be munching. His dark, intelligent eyes seemed to look on me quite affectionately when I brought Mimosa's now somewhat scratched saddle across to him. As I tightened the girths he blew into my hair, then took a strand and pulled it.

"Ow!"

"Steady on, don't shout, you'll frighten him," complained Fergie.

"Well, if it was *your* hair! No, Solitaire, it is *not* funny."

"Those ponies are becoming almost human," said our mother, looking over the fence. "I've brought some carrot peelings for the invalid. Ping Pong! Here, come on, my love. You poor little thing, stiff, are you? Well, I'm not surprised."

Solitaire seemed quite happy to have me on his back, and so relaxed that after a while Fergie led him once round the yard.

"So far so good. Now what about lunging in the field?"

"All right," I agreed, sliding from the saddle, "but first a bit of banging around."

I pulled the stirrups up and down, loosened and tightened the girths, thumped the saddle, and actually crawled underneath Solitaire, while he stood looking completely unconcerned, his underlip drooping a little. Then I led him out into the field and lunged him in the corner, first at the walk and trot and then at the canter on a longer rein. All went well, and I brought him back to the barn feeling just a little triumphant and very relieved.

Next we backed Hopscotch, who was as calm as an old cow attached to a milking machine, and then Jigsaw, who stiffened a little and flashed back his ears, but eventually relaxed and began to nibble at hay while I was on his back.

Then it was lunchtime and we went in to lay the table and help Mum dish up. We had risen at seven and felt well pleased with the amount of progress we had made in one single morning.

During the afternoon after washing up, we lunged all the other ponies, except Ping Pong, in the field, but only managed to persuade Patience to canter—the little ones merely trotted faster and faster until they were horribly unbalanced. Then we asked Dad to drive the mini-bus up and down past the stockyard and afterwards brought the ponies out, one by one, to sniff it. Only Jigsaw and Ping Pong were nervous.

On Sunday morning we turned Solitaire and Patience out into the field and laughed as they rolled on the still-green autumn grass. Mimosa and Silverstar watched from the other side of the hedge, their heads very high, their nostrils dilated. Then a mad gallop began with our two own ponies and Noodles tearing round with their tails very high, attempting to piaffe and passage with wild snorts exploding from their nostrils.

Patience and Solitaire competed on the other side of the fence, the grey gelding's tail held the highest of them all, flying out like a banner. With every stride you could see the Arab blood in him, the showiness, the spring, the wonderful carriage, while Patience moved with a quieter grace, smoothly like a deer, as though confident of her beauty.

"They really have quality. Mastermind was Welsh, wasn't he, so their dams must have had other breeding. I wonder what happened to *them*," mused my brother. "But oh! Aren't you glad that we've saved them from the abattoirs? But for us, someone might now be eating one of Solitaire's ribs—a nice little grilled chop. It doesn't bear thinking about, does it?"

"We haven't won all the way yet," I reminded him. "Now I want to back Tiddly-Winks. I meant to ride her first."

It was a wonderful day that Sunday; everything went well. We rode all the ponies, except for Ping Pong, in the stockyard, and then we took Hopscotch and Jigsaw out for a ride, leading them from Mimosa and Silverstar, and they calmly faced the few cars we met and only shrank a little when a noisy motorbike overtook us at speed, belching dirty, smelly smoke. Patience and Solitaire allowed themselves to be caught in exchange for a handful of oats each, so we decided it was safe to leave them out all night. Our mother spent much of the afternoon with Ping Pong, whom she had taken under her wing, being especially sympathetic towards invalids. She led the little grey to see the hens, and then round the village, saying that she needed to loosen up.

The next evening we lunged each other on Solitaire and Patience at the walk and trot, beginning to teach them the aids, turning them into the centre, stopping and starting. They had already learned to make these movements when asked verbally, which meant we could combine voice, hand and leg, as well as the more subtle use of body weight, to make ourselves understood.

Then on Tuesday we rode them loose in the field as well. Time was horribly short as the nights closed in, but we managed to lunge the others and ride all except Ping Pong in the yard.

"We're really making progress now," said Fergie. "Six weeks doesn't seem such a ridiculous target as it did three or four days ago."

The next evening we reminded ourselves that we had now owned the ponies for a fortnight exactly. It was raining, with thunder rumbling in the distance and the hilltops hidden in dark cloud. The little brown river rushed over boulders and Dad's cattle stood under the trees, patiently chewing the cud. Leerie, fearful of the storm, went indoors. We caught Patience and Solitaire, put them in the barn, rubbed them down and started to teach all the ponies stable manners and prepare them for the blacksmith, picking out their hooves and tapping them with a hammer, and pulling their legs forward as though we were about to use an tripod. Then we found an old sheet of corrugated iron and banged it, to accustom them to noise. Solitaire snorted, Patience moved into a corner, Ping Pong rushed against the fence, Jigsaw stiffened but held his ground. Tiddly-Winks went on nibbling hay as though we were not to be taken seriously, and brave Hopscotch came nearer to see just what we were up to. We bridled each pony in turn, which took a bit of time because we had only two bridles and adjustments had to be made for different head sizes, and taught them to move back when asked. Then we spent ages, with the electric lights on, brushing out their tails and shortening their forelocks. We left Patience and Solitaire in the field for the night and went to bed well pleased.

CHAPTER NINE

THE SECOND SETBACK

The next evening Fergie came back from school in a gloomy frame of mind. Everything, he said, had gone wrong, and he was sure that he had done badly in a test which would decide which sort of examinations he would take at the end of his last year.

A buff envelope awaited us on the hall table. It was a bill for five pounds for the hall we had hired for the jumble sale.

"We can't pay it," said my brother at once. "We already owe Dad nearly forty pounds. We should have charged for entrance, everybody else does. Why didn't we think of it? Then at least we would have got fivepence from the horrible person who stole the radio."

"No one told us," I replied. "And it's all past. No use crying over spilt milk."

"Our parents should have known."

"Why?"

"Well, they're grown-up, aren't they?"

It was raining again. The trees were dripping and the slates on many of the cottages were shining like wet tarmac, and Leerie was soaked.

"No point in catching Patience and Solitaire in this weather. Let's concentrate on the ones in the barn," suggested Fergie, dumping his schoolbag, which had split, in the hall.

"Jake's brought a couple of rubber snaffles," said Mum, coming downstairs. "He says this will be gentler on the ponies' mouths in the beginning, until they understand the aids."

"Oh, how kind!" I said. "He thinks of everything."

"He says you're only to use them when you're riding. Otherwise, if you leave the bits in while the ponies are in the barn, they may chew them. The rubber is very soft. He bought the bits twenty years ago, and hasn't used them much since."

"What are we going to do about this five pounds bill?" asked Fergie. "I don't suppose the hall committee will want to wait four or five weeks. I mean, knowing we are not adults in the full sense of the word, the manager might get suspicious."

"Och, give it to me, if it's only five pounds I'll stand you that—it's not much to ask," said our mother, holding out her hand.

"But I thought you wanted a new pair of jeans," objected Fergie.

"They can wait," she said, "just a few weeks. It's no matter."

"Thanks, thanks a thousand, but we'll pay you back," we said.

After reviving ourselves with biscuits, we went out to the barn. "I feel sick of the whole enterprise tonight," Fergie grumbled. "It seems to be taking so long."

"I'm not. I'm enjoying every minute," I countered smugly.

"Girls always do," said Fergie morosely. "Pony crazy."

"Are you having girl trouble at school?" I asked, feeling concerned.

"No, of course not," he said. "Don't be mad."

The effect of the peat was wearing off and the stock-yard was now very squelchy underfoot. As we crossed it, we could see the four little ponies in the barn.

"They are so small, and I look ridiculous on Hop-scotch," complained my brother.

"The vet comes tomorrow to take Ping Pong's stitches out," I said.

"Don't remind me of that, I can't bear it," pleaded Fergie, "and that will mean another bill, too, and where's all the money coming from? We shall have to advertise and sell one of the ponies soon, just to keep going."

"Nonsense," I said. "You're losing your nerve."

Jigsaw whinnied, his bright little eyes now fully visible since we had shortened his forelock, and his blaze even more endearing in its entirety, the ridiculous, slightly jagged effect giving his face character.

"No sugar today," I said, "just carrot peelings."

"And we owe Dad money for the hay and oats," continued Fergie, whose gloom seemed unbounded.

"He said he wouldn't charge, don't you remember, dismal Desmond? Why don't you snap out of your depression!" I cried, fed up at last with his mood.

"If you weren't a girl I would hit you," said my brother, glowering. "I've had enough."

To my amazement, he turned on his heel and went indoors. I sat down in the straw and the ponies gathered round me as though I was about to tell them a story. I decided to ignore my brother.

"It's wet and you're bored," I said. "Well, let's practice grooming, shall we? Fergie's in a sulk. But we won't take any notice."

I fetched a dandy brush, a body brush and rubber curry comb, which could also be used as a sort of sweat scraper, and set to work.

"Maybe I was a pony in my last life," I said, "because somehow I feel surprisingly at home when I'm with you all, as though I'm part of the herd."

They didn't understand, of course, but Jigsaw took my arm and tugged at the sleeve, and Tiddly-Winks started to chew the body brush.

When I went indoors for supper, Fergie's record player was on full blast as though he wanted to annoy our parents. His bedroom door was firmly shut and a cardboard, handwritten notice pinned to the wood read: *GO AWAY. KEEP OUT. PRIVATE.*

"What *is* the matter?" I called.

"Turn it down, Fergie," yelled Dad, who had just returned, "do you hear?"

"I don't know what's wrong. He's in a terrible mood. Something must have happened at school. Do you know what, Sandy?" asked Mum. "Supper's ready."

"Turn it off!" shouted Dad. "It's time to eat. How can he like that stuff? No tune, no rhythm, no cadence, nothing. Why jazz . . ."

"Oh yes, go on about it!" cried Fergie, appearing at the top of the stairs. "You don't like anything I enjoy, full stop."

"My love, whatever is the matter? You look very redfaced," exclaimed our mother, suddenly concerned. "Are you ill?"

"I've got a headache, that's all, had it all day."

"Why didn't you say?"

"Well, lots of people have headaches, and anyway I didn't think anyone would be interested."

"Now you're being stupid," said Dad. "And that pop won't do the ache any good."

"Tact please, James," said Mummy. "Where's the thermometer? Fetch it, please, Sandy."

Fergie's temperature was 103 Fahrenheit.

"Bed for you, boy," said Dad. "Double quick! I'm sorry I shouted!"

The next morning Fergie showed no improvement, so Mum rang the doctor, and I went to school alone, bitterly disappointed because we had planned that we should take Solitaire for an hour's hack that evening, with Fergie on Silverstar. The rain had gone, the sky was gloriously blue and the air fresh, without any of the mellow heaviness of autumn. Stubble fields lay pale under the October sun; hedges were beginning to turn, brightened by red holly berries, orange hips and haws and the dark elderberries which my mother intended to pick for wine. There were brambles, too, their leaves tipped with yellow and pink, bowed down by the fruit they bore. I wanted to be out

61

riding. I was tired of the yard, of our paddock and the little lanes about the village. I wanted to go further to where fields stretched to meet the sky and unknown tracks led to new adventures. And just at that moment Fergie had to go down with flu! I decided I would not be beaten. I didn't need my brother. I could stand on my own feet.

Caught in one of those mad, irresponsible moods which possessed me sometimes, I suddenly thought: *to the devil with everything, I'm going to ride Solitaire! He's quiet* enough. And, walking home from the school bus stop, my heart lightened and my resentment evaporated. All would be well after all.

"The doctor thinks it's only influenza," Mummy told me, standing on the doorstep, with a jade-green apron tied at the waist.

"Good, that's a relief, but it's going to put us back a bit with the ponies," I said. "It's another setback, and supposing I catch it?"

"Let's face that when it comes, shall we? Aren't you going to ask how he is?"

"Yes, of course. Only I wish he could have avoided being ill just now. I know I sound unsympathetic, but . . ."

"You can't choose when you're going to be ill. If his temperature isn't down by tomorrow, he may have to undergo blood tests."

"Some long illness?"

"Not necessarily, but he may need an antibiotic. Oh look, here's the vet; he's come to take out the stitches."

Ping Pong was very good, because, although no one likes having stitches removed, she only ran backwards a couple of times, otherwise standing patiently.

"Quietening down a bit then," the young vet said. "The scars won't be too bad, although her knees will always be marked."

"You mean she's broken knee-ed?" I asked.

"Afraid so."

"Which means she won't win prizes as a show pony?"

"Well, it will cut back her chances a bit. There you

are, little sunshine. Don't do it again. Next time you see a truck, stop!"

When the vet had gone I tacked-up Solitaire, using a rubber bit.

"I'm taking you out," I told him, "for a little ride all by yourself. So please be good!" I mounted him outside the stockyard, and, without telling anyone, set off. His stride was long, his head high, his sharp ears pricked. Exceptionally intelligent, he already understood the elementary aids, and would trot to a squeeze of my calves, and halt when I tightened my hands and stopped moving with him. I felt very confident, like a queen, up there looking over the tops of the hedges on a pony that moved like a dream. Possessed by a wild sense of bravado, I began to sing *Don't Cry For Me Argentina*, without, I regret to say, a thought for my poor brother sweating it out in bed.

Solitaire had a splendid stride, and he looked about him so that I felt he was enjoying the ride. Every now and then he cocked back an ear to listen to my singing. I went past the turning to Jake's place, and then, half a mile on, took a track that led away from Wales towards the Craven Arms and far away I thought I could see the milder hills of Herefordshire. The sun was going down; the light was changing all the time with the lengthening shadows, and cocks were crowing for the last time before going with their wives to bed in the little houses that some of the cottagers had for their fowl. I was very happy up there alone with the English fields stretched out below, dotted with trees and buildings, with brown patches here and there where a plough had turned the earth.

I patted Solitaire's neck, faintly flecked with varying shades of grey, and admired his darker mane which was beginning to lie neatly on the right side, and I told him that he was wonderful, intelligent and very co-operative. Indeed, I marvelled at his good nature and composure, which made it hard to realise that this was the first time he had been out on his own.

When the track took us between two hedges I urged him

63

into a trot, and then it happened—so swiftly that for a moment I was unaware of the cause. One second we were trotting and the next he was in the air; a twist of his body brought him round until he was facing the other way. But I wasn't. Somewhere I was left behind. I slid; I slipped. I saw the ground rising up to meet me and heaved myself round in an attempt to land on my feet; but when I finally hit land, one foot was twisted under me: a pain shot through my ankle like a tongue of fire. The nut hedge seemed to draw away, to recede into the distance, a faint mist clouded my vision and the next moment I fainted.

"Head between your knees," I thought, coming round. "For heaven's sake—you'll lose your horse." And then I saw the cow on the other side of the hedge, just settling on her feet, slowly, laboriously, and I realised that it was her sudden decision to get up, half hidden from us, which had startled Solitaire. And where was he now? Out of sight, my eyes told me. Gone away. I tried to get up, only to feel the pain returning to my ankle. Was the wretched thing broken? I couldn't get off my rubber riding boot to see. I crawled a few yards then struggled to my feet and started hobbling, but the pain was awful, and every few minutes I had to stop, because the hedge was receding again, and I knew I might faint.

Stumbling along, I cursed myself for being an impatient fool. *More haste less speed* was a maxim drummed into me from early childhood. What would my parents and Fergie think when they found that I had ignored it and gone out alone on Solitaire? This nagging question, in addition to my remorse for not having visited my ill brother before leaving, made me sick with misery. And with the pain biting into my ankle I felt near tears.

The track seemed endless, my painful progress unbearably slow. The skies darkened, the last cocks crew; twilight crept across the landscape, blurring images, the birds became silent in the trees. Night threatened like a heavy hand on the shoulder. Down in the valley a few lights came on, twinkling golden as stars from little windows, making me long for home. What would they be doing down there? Looking for me? Talking of me? Wondering? Dad, seeing that Solitaire had gone, would search for me along the tracks and lanes we normally used. He would not expect me to take this new way which for some reason we had not previously explored. And where was my good grey mount who had gone so well until the old cow had decided to move? Cut and bleeding on the road like Ping Pong?

"Oh!"

I cried aloud as I tripped over, a stone; the pain shooting up my leg, a second burning tongue of fire. Was my ankle broken? The thought numbed me. Six weeks in plaster would mean I could play no further part in breaking-in the ponies, and Fergie was really too tall to ride Tiddly-Winks and Jigsaw. His feet would be just below their elbows, although their backs would be strong enough to take his eight stone. Mrs. Wellbeloved might ask for her money back and without me how could the ponies be sold in time? As I scrambled up again, failure stared me in the face, cold and grey as a frost-bound day. For a ridiculous moment I thought I did not care whether I lived or died. Then I pulled myself together and hobbled on, as the moon, pale and fragile as a wraith, rose in the steely sky. At least I knew the way and had only to retrace the steps I had made so merrily on Solitaire earlier that evening. The track was uneven where a tractor had left deep ruts and twice I tripped, fell again and lay for a moment with the sweat running coldly down my face and the earth damp and unforgiving against my cheek.

"It's all your own fault," I said, "for breaking family rules and going out without telling anyone. You have only yourself to blame!" Then, as if to make myself more miserable, I began to wonder how Fergie was. I saw him in his room, with its cut-out pictures of ships and aircraft, diagrams of the human anatomy and two pin-up girls covering the walls. I saw him feverish, his cheeks flushed, his eyes burning like little blue flames, his hands picking at his blue duvet. I saw our mother hovering, grey-faced

C

and anxious. And I heard my father saying, "Where's Sandy, for heaven's sake? What does she think she's doing, going off into the wilds on a half-broken pony without saying anything?"

I shook myself. My imagination had become more real to me than reality. Besides, the track was running downhill now and my descent would need all my concentration if I was not to fall again. Clouds had moved up from the north-east, hiding the top of the lumpy brown hill that stood behind our house; the moon, too, had gone as the sky turned to charcoal. Shutting out the horrible images of my imagination, I started my descent, sliding on my bottom, trying to guard my ankle, with my head aching and suddenly my eyes smarting. Soon my jeans were wet, and torn by rougher stones, but the road was nearer, and I could see the lights of passing cars, and then the roofs of houses and the electricity poles on which we had stuck the advertisements for the jumble sale. Sheep were bleating and somewhere a bulling cow bellowed forlornly into the night. Then a pony neighed. One of ours? Somebody calling for Solitaire? My hopes rose. Perhaps he had gone home? Perhaps I could count on him to do the sensible thing. At last I came to flatter ground, and I scrambled to my feet again with the gentle murmur of our river in my ears. A rabbit scurried away with bobbing scut. A bat passed by my face, too quick to touch. Bats, I thought. Why were people so frightened of bats? They are like little mice with wings and the old tales about them getting caught in people's hair are untrue, because they have radar systems. They are beautifully equipped. We should admire them. Admire them, yes admire them. I pulled myself up with a jerk as I felt exaggerated tears of pity for bats, rising to my eyes, which was extraordinary.

"Hold on, Sandy," I said aloud, wanting the reassurance of the sound of my voice. "You're getting unbalanced."

Then I came to the road, and collapsed on the verge, clasping my throbbing ankle. Lights from a car shone on the upper lane. The darkness thickened, but I could still see quite well. For a moment I thought I heard a voice calling my name. "Yes, here!" I shouted. Then I decided it had been a delusion. I'm going a bit cracked, I thought. Surprising how silly one gets after a bit of pain. I got up again and started to hobble down the road towards home, which was only just over half a mile away.

CHAPTER TEN

WE SHALL NEVER DO IT NOW

I found progress along the road easier, and, hobbling quickly, was soon home. The hall light was on, the curtains drawn. The scent of roses hung on the night air. I pushed open the door.

"I'm back!" I called, feeling as limp as a wrung-out dishcloth, yet also warm and damp with sweat. The headache still pricked behind my eyes and hammered in my head.

"Hullo, I'm back," I called again and noticed the plaintive tone that had crept into my voice. "It's me, Sandy." Leerie appeared, wagging his feathery tail, smiling with his eyes, and, putting an arm round his neck, I smelt his fur, which was fragrant like wool when it has been washed and not yet dried.

Then Dad's voice bellowed, "Sandy, is that you? Where in heaven's name have you been?"

"Lost. I've hurt my ankle." The plaintiveness had increased almost to a wail.

"Your mother has been scouring the countryside," said Dad, coming through from the kitchen. "Solitaire's back. Hughie, Sandy's here," he added, calling up the stairs.

"Och, is she indeed?" replied my mother in the tight little Scottish voice she uses when she's really angry. "I hope she has a fine excuse for going out on a half-broken pony without telling anyone."

I sat down, for suddenly I felt weak at the knees.

"I'm sorry," I said, as my mother came down the stairs, a little worry line deep at the top of her admirably straight nose. "It was crazy, but now I'm hurt. Is Solitaire all right?"

"Och, yes, the wee pony is fine. He raised the alarm," my mother said, coming close to look into my face. "I went out in the Mini to look for you."

"I hurt my ankle." As I spoke, the hammering in my head increased.

"I expected to find you unconscious," my mother went on. "I kept calling and calling and there was no reply."

"I'm sorry," I said again, while trying to collect my wits, "but everyone falls off sometimes, you must accept that. I don't know why you always imagine the worst. I've got back in the end, although it's taken a long time. I can see in the dark, you know I can see in the dark. I've always been able to see in the dark."

"Such awful things happen at night," my mother said.

"Only very occasionally," I argued, despite the pain in my head. "How's Fergie?"

"Well, it's a particularly virulent bug, and doctor says he must take it easy for a little longer. He's on an anti-biotic; his tonsils are all spotty, but it isn't measles, and his temperature is beginning to drop."

"And what have you done with Solitaire, please?"

"He's out in the field."

"He wasn't frightened?"

"No, he seemed quite calm and collected," my mother said, watching me with strong blue eyes. "Does the ankle hurt much?"

"A bit," I said.

"We had better take the boot off and have a look," suggested Dad, more kindly. "Come on."

"Steady," I said. "The beastly thing is swollen. No, no, that hurts! Stop!"

"You're too rough and impatient, James," said Mum. "Let me try." But she failed, too. So Dad took the carving knife and cut off the boot, and I thought, now who will want to buy me a new pair?

"It doesn't look very happy," commented Mum, gently turning back my sock to inspect the ankle more closely.

"Have you any feeling in the toes? Can you wriggle them?"

I could.

"It's just when I put weight on it," I explained. "Then the pain's rather bad. No, don't touch it, that hurts too."

"Shall we take her to casualty now or wait till morning, what do you think, James?"

Dad said he didn't think we should bother the hospital at this stage. He would run me to the doctors' surgery tomorrow first thing. "Meanwhile, what about embrocation?"

Despite a good meal, bandaging, aspirins and embrocation, my headache was worse when I went to bed, and tears were near. Fergie, struggling with his bug, was not very sympathetic, and although he said, "Bad luck!" he didn't sound as though he meant it.

"You didn't hit your head, did you?" asked Mum. "And you were wearing your crash cap?"

"No, yes. I almost fell on my feet, my feet," I said.

"Why are you repeating yourself?"

"I don't know. I expect I'm very tired," I said, snuggling down in bed. "It's good to be back."

My parents kissed me goodnight. "I'm sorry I shouted at you," Dad said. "But really you must let us know next time when you go riding alone. This accident just underlines the good sense of our rule. We could have found you in a trice if we had known where you'd gone."

"Yes," I said. "I know, I know. Never again."

I had horrible dreams, all concerned with the ponies. Solitaire grew to sixteen hands, turned piebald with the head of a carthorse, Jigsaw fell into a pit and Ping Pong disappeared. I woke up sweating yet cold, with a hammer banging away in my head. My throat was sore, and my eyes hurt. A thin splinter of light slipped through the gap between my curtains. Mummy's big red cockerel crowed; a car changed gear on the road; the world was coming to life. I moved my leg. Pain jabbed at my ankle, and then,

70

because I felt miserable and defeated, I hid my head under the blankets and indulged in a private cry.

"It's half-past seven. Mum is up getting breakfast. She said to ask if you wanted an egg."

I had fallen asleep again and now Fergie was at my bedside, his hair ruffled from the pillow, his blue eyes still a little hazy with sleep.

I rubbed the tears away with my hands.

"Are you better?"

"Yes, the antibiotic is beginning to work. The bug is in retreat. It's incredible how efficient medical drugs are. My headache has gone. But we'll never do it now. Not if your ankle is broken. You were a bit dim, Sandy, truly you were."

"Reckless rather than dim," I said, half sitting up.

"You look a trifle odd. Is the pain very bad? Have you been crying?" My brother turned away to draw back the curtains. "Well, do you want an egg?"

"I've got your bug," I said.

"Oh no, not that!"

He came back to the bed to feel my brow. "You look feverish. I'll fetch the thermometer."

My temperature was 103 Fahrenheit.

"What a bore," said Fergie. "I'll go and break the bad news. No egg, then?"

"Nothing but squash," I told him. "My head is terrible."

Later, before Mum went off to the infant school where she taught, there was a brief family conference in my room, with Fergie trying to speak authoritatively, on account of his medical ambitions, and Dad refusing to take his comments seriously because of his youth. It was eventually decided that I should not now go to the casualty department of the local hospital, because of my temperature and the chance that I might infect other patients. Instead our local doctor would be called.

He came after lunch, a brisk little Welshman full of

jokes, who eventually decided that my ankle was almost certainly only wrenched, bruised and sprained.

"That can be as painful as a break," he explained. "But it mends faster. Normally I would have it X-rayed, just to be sure, but we can't do that while you're fighting this virulent bug, so my verdict must stand for the next few days." As he talked he bandaged my ankle very tightly.

"We'll give you plently of support and then you must try to walk on it. Nowadays we don't rest sprains like these. We keep the joint working to stop it stiffening up. But no riding, mind, not until the pain's gone. Now I must give you a prescription for more antibiotics—you can have a couple of your brother's to go on with. A bit of bad luck having two things at once, isn't it?"

"As long as there's not a third one," said Dad, "we shall survive . . ."

The doctor examined Fergie and announced that he was mending nicely. "If the temperature stays down for the full twenty-four hours, then you can go out."

The rest of the day was dull, because being ill is dull. Unable to read, I was simply waiting to get better, for the headache to go, and for my brain to feel sharp and receptive again. Fergie spent the whole afternoon cleaning tack. Then he prepared tea for everyone. Tigger sat on my bed, purring and pummelling me with his paws, drawing his claws in and out with the regularity of a clock, and Leerie came up at mealtimes, to see whether I could spare him a morsel. The antibiotics soon started to work and by evening my temperature had dropped to just over 101 degrees, so I left bed to watch a television programme. My ankle hurt terribly at first but seemed to loosen up a bit when I walked on it.

And so another day was over and that left only a month, which made us feel a little agitated.

"You must write to Mrs. Wellbeloved and tell her how you're getting on," our mother told us.

"You mean *not* getting on," Fergie said.

Our parents announced we could each take two days off

from school to convalesce from 'flu, so the next day but one Fergie briefly rode all the ponies, except Ping Pong, in the field.

"I agree with you," he said afterwards. "Solitaire is a lovely ride and since he's one of the eldest, at five and a half, we ought to sell him first."

"But if we school him more we can ask a higher price," I argued. "He has the greatest potential. If we sell him too soon we won't reap the full benefit of that."

"Keep walking on that foot, for heaven's sake, we can't do without you. I can't ride them all every day, they're much too small," said Fergie, deeming it wise to change the subject.

CHAPTER ELEVEN

TWO WEEKS TO GO

The blacksmith came with a gas cylinder with which to make a fire to heat the shoes he had brought for Solitaire and Patience. He beat these on an anvil and sang while he worked, and all the ponies liked him, sniffing his leather apron and running their muzzles through his hair. He smelt of hooves and other horses and spoke to them in a soft voice like a gently-flowing river. Solitaire at first hated the smoke and the acrid smell of burning hoof when the hot shoes were fitted against his feet, but Patience, having watched Solitaire, stood quietly and only occasionally looked anxious. The blacksmith rasped the other ponies' feet and measured them for shoes and gave Silverstar removes, and went away promising to be back one day to do the rest. Mummy paid his bill for us, and we made a note of the debt we owed her.

Sensing our desperation and knowing our need to make up for lost time, our parents decided to extend the two days to three to take us to half-term, saying the fresh air and outdoor exercise would build up our strength again. So there were eight glorious days of riding. We backed Ping Pong without a saddle and started to ride the others out in pairs. The weather was fine again and people talked of an Indian summer, and my sprained ankle improved daily. Now all the ponies were living out in the field, and one day Dad cleaned out the yard and sold all but two sacks of manured peat to a market gardener for ten pounds, which he gave to Mum in part payment for the money she had lent us for the blacksmith, which was generous because he had spent something on the peat in the beginning. The two remaining sacks he took to the man who had put the cobwebs on Ping Pong's wounds.

Jake had warned us that at some point there would be a battle between us and the ponies.

"There always comes a time when they want their own way," he had counselled. "It's natural, isn't it? Ponies are spirited animals. The young 'uns always reach a point when they say *no, shan't.* Just like a child, see, and then you have to prove you're boss. You nip it in the bud before it builds up into something big."

Surprisingly, Patience was the first rebel, refusing one day to leave the yard. Flashing back her ears, she stopped and went into reverse. "Walk on," commanded Fergie. "Walk on." But instead of doing so the brown mare swung round and dashed back into the yard. Using his legs hard, Fergie repeated his order, but Patience's expression was one of stubborn determination. She wanted to stay at home with Jigsaw, for whom she had formed a special attachment. Indeed, the little bay whinnied from the field as though they had hatched a plan between them, and Patience answered shrilly.

"A stick," said Fergie. "I shall have to use a stick."

I jumped off Tiddly-Winks, hooked her reins over the fence, which was a calculated risk, rushed indoors and fetched a riding whip, which I handed carefully to Fergie. Then I remounted the little skewbald, who was quite prepared to lead the way out of the yard.

"Walk on," said Fergie sternly. "Walk!"

He used his legs, followed by the stick just behind his left leg, once, twice, and then suddenly the mare bounded down the yard into the road, and the next moment we set off side by side at a brisk trot.

"I'll keep her moving so that she hasn't time to think of a new rebellion," said Fergie. But he wasn't quick enough, for suddenly Patience stopped again, digging in her toes and flinging down her head. Quickly Fergie used his legs and then the stick, and the next minute Patience was cantering. "Whoa, steady, whoa!" Fergie's voice was calm,

75

almost soothing. The battle was won for the moment, and we had no more trouble that day.

Some time earlier, Dad had bought a load of railway sleepers very cheaply, because they were on special offer and seemed a bargain; and, soon after my ankle had recovered, we started walking and trotting the ponies over these in preparation for jumping. In addition we began to lunge them over a couple of cavaletti we had purchased when we had been preparing Silverstar for a show. Jigsaw and Tiddly-Winks showed great promise, but Hopscotch was inclined to cat-jump.

Then, one sunny Saturday, we rode Solitaire and Patience down the lane and through a wood on to a higher road which ran by the forest to Mrs. Wellbeloved's place. These two larger ponies went well together as their strides almost matched and neither had to jog to keep up with the other, but they weren't friends. Patience squealed and stamped if the grey came too close, keeping her affection solely for Jigsaw. Solitaire didn't seem to care. He was a pony who was happy to walk alone; he seemed not to need equine company.

Mrs. Wellbeloved's house stood at the end of an unkempt drive where foxgloves, willow herbs, buttercups and ground elder fought for sustenance from the earth. Garden roses had degenerated into common briars. Virginia creeper and ivy ran rampant over the house, partly obscuring some of the windows, and, strangest of all, a little tree had taken root in part of the slate roof, sprouting cheerfully like a feather from a costerwoman's hat.

My letter to Mrs. Wellbeloved had prompted no reply, and now I began to wonder whether she was ill. The place looked derelict and empty, as though waiting for final demolition. It made me sad to recognise that our benefactor lives in such conditions.

"But perhaps she doesn't care about material things, perhaps she is a saint and only interested in her soul, or a recluse concerned with philosophy and the wicked ways of humanity," suggested Fergie, who was in one of those cheerful and inspiring moods which counterbalanced his times of pessimism.

"She can't be, because she reads the paper and came to our jumble sale. Recluses and saints don't do either. Fancy letting us have so much money when her roof is in such a state. Why, the rain will be in soon."

"Well, maybe she doesn't worry. Her life is nearly over and she's tired of slates and tiles, and builders' men not minding their own business. Here goes!" said Fergie, dismounting to tug the ancient bell-pull.

"So many weeds," I complained. "And tumbledown trees."

"Good for the woodpeckers and wild life in general," retorted my brother. "Tidy gardeners are not good conservationists."

A door opened inside the house, a frail, high voice reached us, "Come on, move, all of you. Fluffy, you'll trip me if you stay there. Pipsy, step aside like a true lady, will you?"

"She cometh," announced Fergie dramatically.

"Oh, shut up, this is important," I said. "We mustn't laugh."

Then the door opened and there stood our benefactor, her face like porcelain in its delicacy and colour, her grey hair wild about her shoulders.

"Oh, it's you," she said, straightening her back and taking on an air of some dignity. "Is the time up already? Have you brought me a cheque? How weeks do fly. It seems but yesterday."

"Two and a half weeks to go," said Fergie, raising his voice.

"There's no need to shout. I may be old, but I'm not deaf," said Mrs. Wellbeloved. "What pretty ponies they are. Wait, I'll get some sugar."

She turned to go back up the passage and seven cats turned with her, all fat, fluffy and well bewhiskered. "These are my children," she said, with a little mocking laugh.

77

"I'm not sure whether they've adopted me or whether it's the other way round."

"I think she could be a saint," I whispered, while Solitaire started to search my pockets for titbits.

The old lady returned with a silver bowl of granulated sugar.

"I had forgotten that they don't sell the lumps in these parts any more. There was no market for them or something," she said. "Nowadays the wishes and needs of the majority always win. The minority is forgotten and yet generally the brains that make a country great are to be found in their ranks. It's all so short-sighted. Now, Pipsy, don't come out. Stay in."

As she spoke, she spooned sugar into her right hand and fed it to each pony in turn.

"We're going to advertise them next week," Fergie told her. "We shall be sad to see them go, but you know we bought them at bargain prices, because the price of live ponies for meat has gone up to £43 a hundredweight. We got these at half that price. Our friend, Jake, says Emlyn Jones was being diddled anyway."

"Really?" said Mrs. Wellbeloved. "That's most interesting. Of course, there have always been rogues in the horse coping business. I remember our groom telling us of a dealer who lamed a horse in three feet so that he would move evenly, as he had an incurable disease in the fourth which made him limp. Wicked, isn't it? Downright wicked!"

"It makes one hate the human race," said Fergie soberly.

"You're looking at my roof!" exclaimed Mrs. Wellbeloved, glancing at me accusingly. "Everyone looks at my roof and I know what they are thinking."

"Just at the little tree, such a brave little tree up there alone," I said whimsically, blushing with embarrassment.

"It's my choice. I have a son to leave the house to but I've had an estimate and it would cost thousands of pounds to put the roof right, and it's not worth all the bother, not to me. I've only a year or two to live, you see. I know;

the doctors have told me. So why bother with roofs and suchlike? Oh, they *are* lovely creatures, aren't they?" She stepped forward to feed the ponies more sugar. "I'm so glad you've saved them from some greedy man's dinner table."

"Or woman's," put in Fergie.

"Yes, or woman's," agreed the old lady, her eyes sparkling a little without losing the faraway look of the very old. "Pipsy come and look at these lovely ponies. Come on, darling. Here Flopsy! And where are Pushkin and Shelley? Come on, puss, puss, puss. I want you all here. Puss, puss, puss." Soon there were seven cats taking turns to purr round her legs, their backs arched, their eyes shining with the curious sensuous intensity of their race.

"Ponies," said the old lady, "See, *ponies.*"

"Patience and Solitaire," I added.

"Supercats," said Fergie, laughing.

"They *are* super," exclaimed Mrs. Wellbeloved. "You've hit on the right word. See how they move. Such elegance! Such grace! That's right, Butterball, take a better look, *ponies.*" We told her that Tigger slept on Hopscotch's back, and she told us about fantail pigeons sleeping on the backs of carriage horses in her youth. And then we said we thought it was time to go, and she said we had been most kind to bring the ponies to see her. The cats had been most interested. And she was very glad that the legacy had been useful. "Money is there to be used. Never forget that," she said. "Don't hoard it. Misers are unhappy people."

Fergie said there was little chance of that happening. We were spenders rather than savers.

"We owe more than money to you," I added. "You gave us encouragement at the right moment."

"Oh, get along with you!" she said with a quick smile. "Well now, if you will excuse me, I must go and wash up. The cats and I have only just finished breakfast. We rise rather late these days."

"Of course," we said. "Thank you for seeing us."

"Come along, Pipsy, Flopsy, my darling Butterball, you roly poly thing. And where are my poets? Shelley, Pushkin! *Milk*, darlings, *milk*."

She turned with all the cats following her, their tails up. And, although we shut the door after her, we thought we could still hear her voice as we rode away down the drive.

"Thank heaven for old ladies who love animals," said Fergie. "What would we do without them."

"Some people would call her a mad eccentric," I retorted cheerfully.

"When I'm a doctor I shall recommend all females over the age of seventy to take in cats. They are the perfect company for someone like Mrs. Wellbeloved," said Fergie. "I see nothing wrong in the old becoming peculiar. At least Mrs. Wellbeloved has something to live for."

"And now what about a gallop?" I asked. "We have only two weeks to go and we haven't tested the ponies' speed. There's a stubble field not far from here, which I saw from the school bus."

"We could have a race," suggested Fergie. "Or would that hot them up too much?"

"We could calm them down afterwards with lots of slow canters side by side," I said. "I bet Solitaire is faster than Patience."

"Bet he isn't."

It was a crisp day with the first hint of winter in the air and a sharp wind whipping our cheeks when we trotted. The leaves were beginning to fall and crackle underfoot, and there was a smell of bonfires in Mrs. Wellbeloved's village.

At the edge of the stubble field we lined the ponies up.

"Ready, steady, go!"

We were off, with the wind stinging our eyes and the thud of hooves in our ears.

"Come on, Solitaire!"

I was forward above his neck; my weight in the stirrups, my hands reaching nearer to his mouth. His feet were pounding faster and faster as the intoxication of the race excited him. Beside us, with flattened ears and stretched neck, galloped Patience. Faster and faster we went, louder and louder seemed the hooves on the cream stubble which was not as soft underneath as we had expected. On the road, which ran parallel, a driver wound down a window to lean out and shout "Tally ho!" Then he overtook us and disappeared into the distance. The green wedge of wood for which we were heading drew nearer and became more distinct. Trees stood out as individuals, shafts of light shone through the branches. And still we rode side by side, our ponies straining every muscle to take the lead.

"Patience, come on, Patience," pleaded Fergie, using his legs but not his stick. Their breath was steamy in the sharp air, their nostrils dilated; then the brown began to draw ahead, first by a muzzle then by a head and soon by a neck. The wedge of wood was beside us now. Solitaire's flanks were heaving. I could hear his breath coming in and out as his sides pumped like bellows, I straightened my back a little, tightened my hands on the reins and he began to come back to me.

"You've won, by a neck," I called. "Solitaire's had enough. I don't want to break his wind."

But Patience wasn't willing to stop. She went on at full speed until Fergie started to turn her in a circle.

"Huh!" he said, coming back at a jog. "She's a galloper—must have thoroughbred blood. It's a pity she's too small to race."

We dismounted and turned the ponies' heads to the wind. We loosened their girths and rubbed their sweaty necks with bits of straw left over by the combine harvester.

"We mustn't do that too often," said Fergie, "or Patience will become uncontrollable. But didn't she go! Why, I think she's even faster than Silverstar, although she's smaller."

"Let's lead them to the road and then mount and go home," I suggested. "We have all the others to ride, and we must draft that advertisement."

CHAPTER TWELVE

SHE NEEDS THE MONEY

"Ponies for sale—yes?" asked Fergie.

"No, *beautiful*, because they are beautiful, aren't they?" I said.

"Well, sort of. It's a pity they've started to grow such heavy winter coats. They're losing their elegance."

"Beautiful Welsh ponies, backed and ready to ride on, isn't that the phrase?" I suggested.

"But Solitaire and Patience have been ridden on quite a bit," argued my brother. "After all, they are promising jumpers."

"But we can't afford a long advertisement," I said.

"Why not *quiet to ride and handle*," put in Dad, who was sitting on the other side of the large kitchen table, writing out bills for some of his mini-bus customers.

"Beautiful Welsh ponies, broken and partly schooled," I said. "How's that?"

"You ought to put in *quiet* somewhere," repeated Dad.

"Well, they're not all that quiet, not yet," said Fergie. "Hopscotch and Tiddly-Winks are, but Jigsaw shies a little and Ping Pong is unreliable; she needs more time."

"And we must add, *some good jumpers*," I murmured, following my brother's earlier line of thought.

"Cut out the *some*," advised Dad. "Never put a word in you don't need."

"All right," I said, writing on the back of a used envelope. *"Beautiful Welsh ponies, broken and partly schooled, promising jumpers, reasonable prices to good homes."*

"Leave out good homes, you can tell the prospective buyers that on the telephone."

"We don't want the meat market men, Dad," I objected.

"Well, they pretend they are buying for good homes anyway. That last sentence won't stop them answering the advertisement," said my father.

"Right," agreed Fergie, "all but the last three words, Sandy. Now, how much will it cost? Remember our telephone number—and we had better put Shropshire in brackets."

We counted the words and next morning Mum bought a postal order and sent off the advertisement to *Horse and Hound* while we were at school.

The nights were closing in fast now and so time was short for us on weekdays. That evening we decided to lunge all the smaller ponies over jumps, which we had built out of cavalettis and sleepers the day before. Ping Pong had marvellous spring but was inclined to cat-jump; Hopscotch didn't like the wider spreads. But they were all willing and not one seemed to refuse out of stubbornness, although occasionally they doubled back for no apparent reason and sometimes we got in a tangle with the lunge rein.

I was in one of those muddles when we heard a car draw up, and then the slam of a door. "Help me, Fergie, please," I said. "Hurry, someone is arriving."

My brother turned round the little bay and set him off again at a brisk trot, and then we saw a figure coming across the field, a golden labrador at her side.

"It's our friend in the green quilted jacket, the jumble sale lady," said Fergie. "I wonder what she wants."

I called in Jigsaw and waved.

"Hi, there," the woman called. "He's going nicely, isn't he?"

"A great little pony," muttered Fergie, who intended to play the part of a salesman.

"I've got a friend who wants a leading-rein pony, so, of course, I thought of you," the woman said as she came up to us. "Sit down, Sandy."

It was a moment before I realised that she was talking to the dog.

"She prefers a grey," the woman went on. "She wants it for show. She has a spoilt little brat of five and a half—you know how it is—but I reckon she would provide a good home."

"We've just finished lunging the grey—she's in the barn," said Fergie.

"She looks beautiful in the photograph," said our friend

"That was the bigger one. We haven't ridden the little one very much because she's too small for us," I explained, walking back across the field.

"Well, she'll be led mostly, so what does it matter? So long as she's beautiful."

As we came to the barn there was a funny feeling in the pit of my stomach and, knowing in advance what the verdict would be, I felt sorry for Fergie.

"Come on, Ping Pong, there's a good little pony." He fetched a handful of oats out of his pocket and slipped on a headcollar. "I'll bring her outside."

"Isn't she exquisite?" the woman said.

"She was even more beautiful in her summer coat." I tried not to look at the scars.

Fergie tried to make Ping Pong stand like a show pony, while our friend attempted to run her eye over her.

"Oh golly, she's marked! You've let her injure herself! She's no use for showing. I'm sorry. Oh, what a shame! She'll never win a lead rein class now. How did it happen? What a tragedy. Sit down, Sandy, at *once*."

Suddenly the woman seemed too critical to be our friend. She made us feel small and hopeless and inefficient.

"She got out on the road," began Fergie, looking horribly guilty.

"And fell and broke her knees, and that's the end of her show career. It really is," the woman went on. "And she's the best of the bunch, the only one for that particular class."

"The skewbald?" I suggested. "She's a better size."

"But they wanted a grey."

"Yes, but other coloured ponies go into leading-rein classes," I said. "The skewbald has better carriage."

"You know this grey would be worth two hundred and fifty as she stands, just backed, *but* for those poor knees," the woman continued relentlessly. "She's a gem."

"Yes," agreed Fergie, leading Ping Pong back to the barn.

"Someone will love her whether she has scars or not," I replied. "Looks are not the only thing that matters."

"But for showing," the woman began again.

"Oh yes, they're a hard lot in the showing world," I said angered and upset for Fergie as well as Ping Pong. "I think we want these ponies to go to nice children who will treasure them whether or not they win prizes."

"You're right, of course," the woman said, "but I'm so desperately disappointed because I did so want to arrange a sale for you."

"Well, accidents do happen and sometimes it's nobody's fault," I retorted, rather too brusquely.

"I'll keep on trying," the woman said. "Better luck next time. Come on, Sandy." She turned towards her car, her face a little red, her grey eyes the colour of herrings.

"Do you want a cup of tea? I mean would you like to come in," I asked.

"No, thank you so much. I'm on my way somewhere. I was just passing."

"Thank you for thinking of us," called Fergie, with a face as long as a lane.

"You haven't let any of the others get marked, have you?" the woman asked, turning back. "You see I might hear of someone else."

"Not so far. We do our best," said Fergie. "I mean, we *do* try to keep them sound and fit."

The *Volvo* throbbed into life. From a window Leerie barked madly at the labrador.

"A bad beginning," I said.

85

"She was tactless," complained my brother. "Why couldn't she shut up?"

Then Dad called to us from the house. "There's been an important telephone call."

We went indoors. "It was Mrs. Wellbeloved's lawyer," he said. "He wants to know how you're getting on, because, he says, she's overlooked some bills, and she'll need the money back for sure on Monday week."

"That allows us eleven days to sell some of them," I groaned. "I just hope the telephone starts to ring first thing Saturday morning. Oh dear, I feel awful!"

"Better phone an advert through to the local rag," suggested Dad. "I'll advance you the money."

"Actually, I don't want them to go at all," I admitted. "I shall cry when Solitaire leaves."

"Don't be a fool, Sandy," said Dad, quite crossly. "You're in debt and you've got to be practical and sensible. Now pull yourselves together."

"We might have sold Ping Pong, if only," began Fergie.

"Oh, don't torture yourself with that," I cut in. "What's the point of crying over spilt milk?"

"I'm only stating facts," said Fergie. "That woman made me feel like a criminal."

CHAPTER THIRTEEN

HE'S THE ONE FOR ME

The first reply to our advertisement came on Friday evening as we were having supper. I answered the telephone.

A child's voice said, "It's about the ponies. How much are they, please?"

"Oh, we're open to offer," I said in a rush, for we had been remiss enough not to have decided what we would charge for each one.

"Offer? Only Daddy wants to know, you see," the child said. "Surely you know."

"Well, between one hundred and fifty and two hundred and fifty pounds," I replied. "About that anyway. It all depends."

"Do sound more business-like," called Dad from the supper table. "Don't be *vague*."

"Hold on, please," the child said.

I put my hand on the receiver to call "Please shut up," in the direction of the kitchen.

"When can we see them?" asked the child in a small voice.

"Tomorrow morning."

"What time, please?"

"About ten o'clock," I replied after a pause, in which I considered how long it would take me to wash and dry Solitaire's tail and groom Jigsaw and Tiddly-Winks. "What size do you want?"

"I don't know, about thirteen hands. I'm ten," the child said. "Can I have the address? We live by Hereford."

"That's not far," I said.

"I didn't think they would start ringing until tomorrow morning," our mother commented when I returned to the kitchen. "I'm glad you've got a nibble straight away. It's a good omen."

We set our alarm clocks and rose at seven the next day. We caught up the ponies and washed the greys' tails before breakfast, and then, after grooming all of them, we gave the tack a wipe over, feeling annoyed with ourselves for not having had the sense and energy to clean it the night before.

Then the telephone rang again, and this time Fergie answered and spoke with a woman who was looking for a family pony of around 13.2 hands with jumping potential. He told her about Patience and Solitaire and she said she would be along at two o'clock with an expert.

He had just put down the receiver when the ten-year-old arrived with a tall, youngish father in gold-ringed spectacles and a red beard.

By this time I had written down prices on a piece of paper.

Solitaire £250.   Hopscotch £200.

Patience £250.   Jigsaw £200.

Tiddly-Winks £200.   Ping Pong ?

Thrusting it into Fergie's hands, I said "O.K?" "More or less," he hissed, as our prospective buyer's daughter came down the path, pulling on a pair of brand new yellow string gloves.

"I'm Stephanie Cann. Who are you?" said the child.

"We're the Hamiltons. I spoke to you last night. I'm Sandy and this is my brother, Fergie."

"Come to the barn," suggested my brother. "All the ponies are there, lŏose but catchable."

"Stephanie is quite fearless," the bearded man said to me in an undertone. "But I am very anxious that any pony she has is absolutely all right with traffic, that's the first essential."

"Well, we live in a quiet place as you see; they don't meet a great deal here," I replied.

"The grey!" cried Stephanie. "I love the grey." She

88

rushed across and threw her arms round Ping Pong's neck.

"She's not ready," said Fergie.

"What do you mean, not ready?" asked the child, glaring. "I thought they were all for sale."

"She's marked," replied Fergie soberly. "See those scars. She took a bit of time to recover, so she hasn't had as much schooling as the others."

He started to saddle and bridle Hopscotch.

"The skewbald is a bit small—you would soon grow out of her—and the bay is a little nervous. He hasn't met double-decker buses, so I can't guarantee him quiet in heavy traffic," I said.

"And this biscuit-coloured one?" asked the bearded man, whose eyes were a strange yellowy brown, almost amber.

"The quietest of the lot, and a good little jumper," I replied.

Fergie vaulted into the saddle and rode Hopscotch out into the field where we'd schooled the ponies.

"He hasn't a very long stride," said Stephanie, beating her left rubber boot with her riding stick, "but I like his eye. Does he have any splints or spavins?"

"I hope not, he's only four and a half. I haven't noticed any, but you're welcome to have him inspected by a vet," I said, thinking that she was remarkably businesslike for a ten-year-old.

"Stephanie reads every horsey book she can lay her hands on; she's a fanatic," Mr. Cann explained, smiling.

"So he hasn't got all his teeth yet," the girl suggested.

"No, the corners are still baby ones," I replied. "Have a look if you like."

"She wants to ride for England, that's her burning ambition," Mr. Cann added, wiping his spectacles.

"He wanders," said Stephanie.

"What, who?"

"The pony doesn't go straight," said Stephanie. "He's not going into his bridle."

"Steady on there, Steph," warned Mr. Cann.

"It's true," she said.

After showing his paces, Fergie jumped Hopscotch over a few cavelettis and then came back to us. "Want a ride?" he asked, dismounting.

"Yes, please," said Stephanie.

"Her head's full of dressage," explained Mr. Cann. "She's been having lessons in a covered school from a top rider."

She rode well, but with more contact on the reins than Fergie used, so that Hopscotch fussed a little.

"He's not quite what I want," she said, coming back after a short walk, trot and canter. "What about the other grey?"

"Solitaire? Isn't he rather big?"

"She'll ride anything," Mr. Cann said. "She's a great girl."

"And if we got on together I would never part with him, not for a million pounds," added Stephanie. "I promise a good home."

So I brought out Solitaire, and he went like a dream, even leading off on the correct leg every time, although I had only started teaching him about leading legs a few days earlier.

I jumped him over two cavelletis piled on top of each other, and our highest obstacle made out of sleepers which was just under three feet, and over an old brush fence which we had put up years ago for Mimosa. And I galloped him to show that his wind was all right.

"*He* goes into his bridle," she said, as I came back.

"Yes, and he's a natural jumper; he's had very little training," I added, feeling a little sick at heart. "It's not six weeks since he was backed."

I legged Stephanie up into the saddle, adjusted her stirrups and advised her not to ride him on a tight rein.

"All right. Yes, I see," she said.

She rode off with a very straight back, her heels well down, and her hands just in front of the saddle. And she looked great. I couldn't refuse to see that she rode well.

She was small for her age, but would grow into Solitaire, and she was firm enough in the saddle to control him, however excited he might be. An infant prodigy, I decided.

She walked, trotted and cantered the grey then jumped him over all the obstacles and came back smiling.

"He's the one for me," she said.

"How much are you asking?" enquired Mr. Cann, looking at me. "Or is that a question we should put to your parents?"

"Three hundred pounds," I announced and saw Fergie's face twitch. "He's the best of the lot. He has tremendous potential," I said, not wanting the Canns to have Solitaire, because I didn't like Stephanie's abrupt manner and reddish hair, not realising until much later that my dislike was based partly on envy. Surely, I thought, they will say the price is too high. Out of the corner of my eye I could see Fergie walking up and down as though under stress. Stephanie jumped from the saddle and put her arms round the grey's neck.

"You're wonderful," she said.

"We'd better think it over," suggested Mr. Cann at last.

"But I know he's right for me," argued Stephanie. "Please, Daddy."

"We'll talk it over with Mummy. Do you guarantee him quiet in traffic, Miss Hamilton?"

"Quiet with tractors and trucks and mini-buses," I answered.

"We don't meet anything worse where we live," said Stephanie.

"We'll ring after lunch," said Mr. Cann.

"We have other people coming to see him at two," put in Fergie.

"Before that, then," said Mr. Cann.

"He won't have to live alone; you've got a nice field for him?" I asked.

"Oh, no, he'll be with my friend's roan and we have a stable next to the house. Daddy's a scientist," said Stephanie, as though that explained everything.

Then she looked at Solitaire's teeth and ran her hands down his legs, and I was forced to admire her efficiency, bearing in mind that she was only ten. At that age I had still been bumping around at a riding school with my reins too long and my toes turned down. Some people seemed to have all the luck!

"Have you got a measuring stick?" she asked.

"Sorry, no, but I think he'll squeeze into the 13.2 and under classes if you allow for the shoes."

"He might still grow a bit."

"You'll have to risk that," I said. "You ought to try him on the road, to make sure he's not nappy."

"He doesn't *feel* nappy," she said, remounting. "But here goes." She rode him round the village lanes, met a tractor and came back even happier. "He's great, fabulous, and worth every bit of three hundred pounds. He might even win a junior hunter class," she said.

"Right, enough is enough. You've had a good trial. We must go and fetch Mummy. Come on now," said Mr. Cann.

When they had gone, Fergie said, "Why on earth?"

"You mean I shouldn't have asked three hundred pounds?"

"Absolutely."

"I don't think I want her to have him. I thought she might be put off."

"It only spurred her on. But I think you're being unfair. I think she genuinely likes him," said Fergie. "It should be a good home. And three hundred pounds would go a long way towards settling our debts."

"I hate asking money for a friend," I said. "I feel like Judas or something."

"Now you're exaggerating," said Fergie. "Ponies are ponies, not people."

CHAPTER FOURTEEN

A FIRST-CLASS HOME WITH MONEY
NO OBJECT

The woman in search of a family pony arrived half an hour later, with four children and an expert wearing jeans and a riding coat. She looked at the ponies one by one and wondered why only two were shod. We explained about the cost, and said that if she wanted to buy one we would have a set of shoes put on before delivery. She said, "Fair enough."

The expert suggested that only Solitaire, Patience and Hopscotch were large enough to meet the family's needs, so, as the Canns had not rung back, we rode those in turn for her to see. Solitaire refused the brush fence for no particular reason and the expert was surprised that I had not taught him to rein-back. Patience was still excited after her race and inclined to throw her head about. The tallest child, a boy, decided both these ponies were too lively for him, but eventually rode Hopscotch who, to our amazement, refused to leave the gate with him.

"He's never done that before," said Fergie.

"There's always a first time," the expert remarked, standing there with her hands in her pockets and a critical expression on her plump face, which was framed by dark curly hair. "I don't think any of them are schooled enough for us. They need more expert children to ride them on."

"Right," said Fergie, looking dismal because of Mrs. Wellbeloved's bills.

"Let's just glance at the rest," the expert suggested. "But these three are lovely ponies; the brown has a smashing front; the grey has a wonderful air about him, and the little dun will be a super first pony when he's gained a bit more experience. You've done well in seven weeks."

We went back to the barn and Jigsaw whinnied a welcome.

"He's sweet," the youngest child said.

"That's rather a super skewbald. Can we see her out?" asked the expert. "Isn't she prettily marked?"

I clipped a rope on Tiddly-Winks' headcollar and led her round the yard and then up and down the drive.

"She's so pretty," the expert said, "let me feel her legs, will you? But give her another trot first. I want to see if her action is absolutely straight, no plaiting or dishing." Sensing the admiration, Tiddly-Winks pranced like a poodle, shook her lovely mane, and held her tail like an Arab.

"She looks even better in a summer coat," I said.

"You know, she's worth a bomb as a leading-rein pony," the expert said after feeling her legs. "Look at that shoulder, and the way she carries herself. She's a winner, no mistake about that. Let's see her under the saddle."

I tacked-up and we returned to the field.

"She's first-class, absolutely," the expert said, after I had ridden for a while. "I should know; I judge the classes sometimes. With a proper straight-cut show saddle and plaited mane, she would be unbeatable."

"That's nice to know," Fergie said, at last. "How much should we ask for her?"

"Well, she'll need more schooling, but honestly I could get four hundred for her tomorrow, as easy ts that," the the expert snapped her rather short fingers.

"Well, please do," urged Fergie, "because we are in debt."

"But only to a good home," I said.

"Oh yes, a first-class home with money no object. Why, the mother is Angela Calloway." I caught my breath at the name of one of the leading show hack riders. "And she wants something really good for her four-year-old son," the expert said.

"Make it four hundred and fifty then," Fergie suggested.

"I'll see and ring you back," the expert promised, patting Tiddly-Winks. "You're a beauty, you are."

"By Mastermind," I said.

"And he won a few prizes as a stallion years ago, I seem to remember," the expert said, kicking the turf with her foot.

"Did he? We don't know," I said. "Perhaps we weren't born."

"Well, about ten years ago, or more."

The children were getting fed up and, after a good deal of muttering, they started to swing on a gate and then to throw stones at the barn wall.

"Home, and better luck next time," their mother said, looking tired and overworked as she ran a hand across her eyes. "I'm sorry nothing was quite far enough on for us, but it's nice that Janet has a buy."

"Thank you for coming," I said.

"A family pony is never an easy thing to find," the expert remarked, getting into the car. "Thank you for showing them to us."

"Want an ice cream!" the youngest child cried. "Mandy hungry!"

"Soon, darling," the mother said, starting the engine.

"Whew!" cried Fergie, as the car drove off. "Do you think Janet What's-her-name meant it?"

"Yes, it could save us and the others. I always said Tiddly-Winks was a pretty pony."

"It looks like two of yours going and none of mine," mused Fergie.

"I'm not sure about Solitaire. I didn't like the girl. Anyway, they haven't rung back."

"I think she was all right," Fergie said. "She rode well, and she was keen."

"Her personality."

"Oh, that's just you. I don't suppose Solitaire will be fussed by that. She was incredible for ten."

We went indoors to tell our parents about the expert's view of the skewbald.

"But have you actually sold anything? Have you got a cheque in your hand?" asked Dad. "Two answers aren't very many and you've really only got to next Wednesday or Thursday, because you must give the cheque four days to clear before you can pay back Mrs. Wellbeloved. The lawyer wants the debt settled exactly eight weeks from the date we signed the document and that's Monday week, that means eight days from now; allow for the clearance and you come down to four days, and, even then, we're taking a risk because we are counting Sunday as a clearance day."

"Oh, Dad," I moaned. "Do you want to give us a sleepless night?"

"They are doing their best, James," our mother said. "Don't be discouraging. You make everything sound so complicated."

"I'm only stating facts," replied Dad. "It's no good burying your heads in the sand; that lawyer chap was pretty firm."

"Mrs. Wellbeloved wouldn't let him prosecute. She would allow us some extra days, I know she would," cut in Fergie.

"And possibly risk jail herself for her debts?" asked Dad.

The next morning, the telephone rang at half-past eight and, thinking it might be Stephanie Cann, I shouted at Fergie to answer. But it was a man who had seen our advertisement in the local paper.

"I just want a little look-see. There may be nothing I like, but those who don't look don't find, do they?"

"No, well, do come along," said Fergie, and then he went on to describe the way.

"Meat man," I cried when my brother had repeated the conversation to me.

"Not necessarily," argued Fergie.

"A dealer, anyway," I said.

"He could be a farmer or corn merchant looking for a pony for his children or grandchildren, one never knows," said my brother. "Now don't get all het up. We can't turn away possible customers just because our imaginations run away with us."

"I bet I'm right. He's not having one of *my* three," I said.

"He's coming straight away, so we had better start catching them up," said Fergie. "Come on, run."

But just as we dashed across the garden the telephone rang again.

"You go!" cried Fergie.

It was Mrs. Wellbeloved, sounding husky, old and rather faint.

"Is that Sandy, the girl with the ponies?" she asked, hesitantly.

"Yes, it's me, er, hullo, how are you?" I asked, my heart sinking a little on account of her solicitor's letter.

"Not very well," she replied. "I expect you received a sort of business letter from my lawyer. Well, I'm just wondering whether you could let me have a little back a bit sooner. I have troubles I haven't mentioned to him. I know you're not legally bound, my dear, but . . ."

"Of course," I said. "We'll do our very best. How much do you need?"

"Could you manage a third in cash?"

"Two hundred pounds?"

I must have sounded aghast, for she said, "I realise it's rather a large sum, but I owe the builder money and he has been round threatening me. You see, I didn't realise my account was so low and I gave my son a little something for a business venture, a thousand pounds. He's such a charmer, my son, and I always give way; he's so persistent . . . Of course I realise now that I should not have done that. You see I'm going a little blind, my dear, and I don't always read the small print, and bank statements are so confusing these days. It's very difficult being old. Shelley, be quiet. If you could bring me two hundred pounds before that nasty man comes back with a summons or something, I should be so very grateful. You do understand, my dear, don't you?"

"Yes, yes. Well, we've almost sold one of the ponies but not quite. I'm sure we can manage."

"The sooner the better," said Mrs. Wellbeloved. "I am sorry I have got myself in such a pickle and caused you so much trouble."

"No, not at all. I must go now. We've got a man coming to look at the ponies in a moment, so I must rush and catch them up."

"Good luck, my dear," said Mrs. Wellbeloved, before hanging up. My legs felt wobbly, and suddenly my body seemed light, as though I had no inside.

It was drizzling and the ponies looked wet and cross, and we couldn't catch Jigsaw. I told Fergie the bad news as we led the others across the field.

"Why do the old make such a mess of things?" he asked.

"Wait until you're eighty and then you'll know," I said.

"Poor Mrs. Wellbeloved," he added after a moment, while he fought back the irritation which had been his first reaction to my news. "How could a builder bully a frail person like that?"

"He wants his money."

"Did you ask his name?"

"No, I'm sorry," I said, feeling inefficient.

"Pity, because we might have popped round to see him and persuaded him to wait."

"I don't know what we can do, if we don't sell a pony today. I mean Mrs. Wellbeloved might take an overdose of sleeping pills in despair. Have you thought of that?" I asked dramatically. In my imagination I saw Mrs. Wellbeloved lying dead on a bed, stretched out on faded patchwork with all her cats mewing around her. "And her pussies will starve before she's found."

"Cats never starve. They're too resourceful," said Fergie firmly. "So do stop piling on the agony. I accept that we are morally bound to produce the two hundred pounds, but let's wait until this guy has been before we start looking on the worst side and letting our imaginations run away with us."

At that moment the man arrived in an old estate car with a trailer, and leaped out with alacrity, words flowing from his mouth softly like a river.

"Quick, wasn't it? I know the place, as a matter of fact. I've lived in these parts all my life. Ah, so these are the ponies—not a bad bunch, are they? The little grey's marked, of course. Broken them in yourselves, have you?"

"Yes, that's right," said Fergie.

"Long-reined them?"

"No, just lunged," I said.

"We reckon you can do everything the long reins do from the saddle, with the added advantage that you can use your legs to keep the ponies up to the bridle," added Fergie.

"Dressage riders are you?" asked the man, looking like an old-fashioned groom in his breeches and gaiters. Then, pushing his cap back on his head, he said, "I'll give you a couple of hundred for the skewbald."

"No, thanks, she's more or less sold for more than twice that," I answered quickly. "She'll make a top-class leading-rein pony."

"You've got your heads screwed on the right way, I can see that," said the man, with a quick smile. "What about that brown mare, she's got a bit of quality about her."

"Yes, she's great," replied my brother slowly. "But you know you haven't told us your name. We're the Hamiltons—and you?"

"Joe O'Rourke."

"From Ireland?" asked Fergie.

"My grandfather was, came over as a groom, but I was born the other side of Ludlow. We've got horses in the blood. Now how about clapping a saddle on the brown? I'd like to see her go. She'll make a nice pony for a child who can ride a bit."

"All right," said Fergie, reluctantly going for the tack.

"She's my brother's favourite," I explained. "He doesn't want to part with her."

"Ah, but he needs something bigger. He'll soon be a man," said Joe O'Rourke, lighting a cigarette. "I know a hunter that would suit him a treat, jumps like a stag and no vices."

"Do you deal in horses?" I asked, as Fergie bridled Patience.

"A little bit, to good homes, people I know. Have they worn keys?"

"What do you mean?"

"Mouthing bits."

"No, we haven't any."

"Side reins?"

"No."

"You've overlooked a lot then, done only half a job."

"Well, our book says it's best to do most of the work from the saddle. Long reining can get a horse behind the bit, and why walk when you can ride?"

"You don't want to take notice of books. It's experience that counts," Joe O'Rourke said, moving out into the yard so that he could watch Patience from the front as Fergie rode her out. "She moves straight. Let's see her on the grass. Got a turn of speed, has she?"

"Oh yes," said Fergie. "She likes a gallop."

"That's the blood in her, you can always tell, breeding will out," the man said.

Fergie showed all her paces, galloped her and put her over the jumps and came back looking as dismal as a criminal going to the dock.

"We only sell to good homes," he said. "Do you want a ride?"

"No, trot her on the road, let's see if she's truly sound," replied O'Rourke. And when that was done he offered us two hundred pounds.

"If you're a dealer, I am afraid it's no," Fergie answered
100

after a long pause. "Unless we can see the people she's going to."

"It's a good sound offer, and you can have it in cash. I can't be fairer than that," said Joe O'Rourke, bringing out wads of notes from his pocket. "There's no one straighter than me."

"She's worth that for meat further south," I said at last.

"I'll make it two hundred and ten then. How's that?" The man asked, beginning to count the notes, which were mainly tenners, as though the sight of money would change our minds.

"Have you anyone in mind for her?" I asked, trying to see a loop-hole which would reassure us so that we could accept his offer and repay our benefactor the money she needed so desperately.

"A young gentleman," replied the dealer at once. "A lovely home, big house with a park, hunters kept. In the Cotswolds. There's a lot of money in the Cotswolds. She'll be out with the Heythrop. They've got a groom, too. You don't need to worry a scrap. She'll be well cared for. The whole place is fenced with timber, not a strand of wire to be seen."

I looked at the money and at the man's weather-beaten face; his brown eyes were soft, like caramel. "I wouldn't let a mare like this go anywhere but to the best. You can trust me. Why, I've been in the trade thirty years and I know a nice pony when I see one." I thought of Mrs. Wellbeloved, waiting in her house with the little tree sprouting from the roof like a travelling umbrella. I saw her surrounded by cats, her boney hands in her lap; her blue eyes focused on the window, her old ears straining to hear the footsteps of the builder; a big burly fellow with a red, threatening face, large cracked hands.

"Do you swear it's a good home?" asked Fergie very sternly.

"Cross my heart, on my honour," replied the man without a moment's hesitation, stuffing the money in his pocket so that his hands were free to caress Patience. "There, my little beauty."

Fergie looked at me, his dark eyebrows raised in enquiry. I nodded. "All right," he said, "in cash then."

It was fate, or perhaps God, I thought, helping us, bringing us the money in the right form just when we needed it. Certainly, it was more than coincidence. Perhaps, on second thoughts, Mrs. Wellbeloved had a guardian angel.

The man counted the notes and handed them to Fergie. "Done," he said.

Patience didn't want to go into the trailer, although it was well bedded down in straw and without a partition so looked quite inviting. But Joe O'Rourke was very patient, lifting her feet up on to the ramp and encouraging her in his soft voice. And after half an hour, she cast us an unforgettably imploring glance before stepping in.

"Put up the ramp, will you?" asked the dealer, "nice and quick, if you don't mind."

And that was that. A few moments later, Joe O'Rourke drove carefully out into the road, and Patience let out a heart-rending whinny which was answered by Solitaire.

"I feel like Judas Iscariot," said Fergie, looking distastefully at the money in his hand.

"It's not for us. It's for poor little Mrs. Wellbeloved," I reminded him.

We went indoors. "Our first sale," said Fergie, throwing the notes down on the kitchen table.

"Good Lord! In cash, too. You don't sound very pleased," said Dad. "Look out, or they'll blow away!"

"Congratulations!" cried our mother coming into the room. "Which one?"

"The best," said Fergie, and I hadn't the heart to contradict him.

"We didn't like the man, but he promised a good home, and we had to have the money. You see, Mrs. Wellbeloved rang." I explained the situation to our parents. "We had better go round straight away with the cash," I finished.

"Oh no, you don't," said Dad. "Old ladies often have

shaky memories. You must get a receipt. Otherwise she might turn round on Monday and, saying you never called at all, ask for two hundred pounds all over again."

"We can easily prepare a receipt," Mum said. "Then she only has to sign."

"No, on second thoughts, leave it to first thing Monday morning, then I can inform her solicitor," said Dad.

"But we shall be at school," objected Fergie, looking despondently out of the window.

"Well I haven't a job till half ten, so I'll do it for you. I'm not saying the old lady is dishonest, only that she's perhaps a little senile and forgetful, and one has to protect oneself in life against forgetful people, especially in business dealings."

"Thanks, Dad, better take the money then," replied Fergie, shoving the pile of notes in our father's direction. "Come on, Sandy, let's go out and do a bit of schooling. We must ride Ping Pong in a saddle and then you had better teach Solitaire to rein-back—after all he's well up to the bit—and we ought to practise turns on the forehand, which will make them all better at opening gates."

In the evening when we were sitting by the fire in the sitting room, doing the last of our homework, there was a knock at the kitchen door and we found Jake standing on the step.

"Just came round to see how things were going, and I brought this little felt saddle, had it years, thought it would do for the smaller ponies."

"Oh, Jake, you're an angel. Do come in. Sit down," I said. "You're right. Mimosa's saddle *is* too big for them and rocks about. This is perfect."

"Just the thing for Ping Pong," added Fergie.

"Made any sales yet?" asked Jake. "Time's getting on for you, and I don't suppose the old lady can wait beyond the agreed date. I've heard tell that she's in financial difficulties and a certain gentleman, if you can call him that, is threatening action, bailiffs or something."

103

"Patience has been sold," said Fergie. "Two hundred and ten pounds."

"The dark brown mare?"

"That's it. So we are taking Mrs. Wellbeloved some money tomorrow," I said.

"Well, you do look down in the mouth to be sure. Who's bought her then?" asked our friend.

We told Jake, and at the name O'Rourke he sat up very straight.

"Not Joe!" he said. "Not Joe O'Rourke?"

I felt as though a cold creature was creeping up my spine. "What's wrong with Joe O'Rourke?" I asked.

"Everything," said Jake. "He's the one who was buying them in the first place."

Fergie whitened. The cold creature seemed to be pushing ice along my spiral cord.

"I'm not saying he'll sell her for meat," continued Jake, "not now someone else has taken the trouble to break her in, so don't go and upset yourselves, but he's not to be trusted. Did he give you a cheque?"

"Cash," we said.

"Is Joe on the telephone?" enquired my brother after a long and mournful pause.

"Couldn't say, don't have dealings with him myself," said Jake. "He lives in Herefordshire."

"He came so quickly, I thought he was near," said Fergie.

"No, he probably had a horse to deliver and rang from there. He never wastes a penny or a journey if he can help it, and he's up with the dawn."

"Where will she go?" asked Fergie desperately.

"To the person who will pay the highest price the quickest," said Jake, lighting a cigarette.

"And if he can't find anyone?"

"To the continent, and after buying at two hundred and ten pounds Joe won't have made a loss."

"On the hoof, as meat?" I asked in a small voice.

"That's it."

"What can we do?" asked Fergie, twisting his hands.

"Buy her back, that's the only thing," replied Jake gravely.

"But Mrs. Wellbeloved . . ." I began.

"You have a bit of time," Jake said. "Joe will try to sell her first at three hundred pounds or so, but with winter coming on he won't wait more than a few weeks. You see, last week horseflesh was selling at £45 per hundredweight on the hoof, so he's well covered financially."

I remembered the imploring look Patience had given us, and felt sick.

"I can see her haunches hanging in a butcher's shop," said Fergie, his blue eyes very hard, like semi-precious stones, with no softness, no soul in their centres.

CHAPTER FIFTEEN

WE MUST BUY HER BACK

Monday came in wet and cold, with a November mist obscuring the hills and a north-west wind bringing down the last of the leaves. We fed the ponies hay in the fields and walked to the school bus stop with heavy hearts, faithful Leerie trotting at our heels.

"Dad will be off with the money soon," Fergie said. "I hope Mrs. Wellbeloved is pleased."

"Why did we let Patience go for so little? What came over us?" I asked.

"A sort of madness. I saw the money as a gift from the gods to help us out of a scrape," said my brother.

"Like me!" I exclaimed. "I thought the same. And I half believed the man."

"He may have a home waiting. He may have spoken some truth, but, all the same, we must try to buy her back as soon as we can. I can't bear not to know where she has gone," said Fergie. "I hardly slept at all last night."

"We won't tell anyone, will we?" I said. "I mean, what could be more awful than the fact that we've sold one of the ponies to the very man from whom we saved them in the first place."

"The only consolation is that he won't take her straight to the slaughterhouse, since she's now worth more as a riding pony, if she can find a home," said Fergie. "When I woke up this morning I wished I was dead."

Then the bus came. "Goodbye, Leerie, take care going back," I patted the collie. "Look after the ponies, there's a good dog."

"Sold anything?" asked Trevor, as we climbed inside.

"One," replied Fergie, "and lots of bites at the cherry."

"Firm bites?" asked Pippa.

"Sort of," I said.

"Big price? Good profit?" asked Trevor.

"Middling," replied Fergie, looking away out of the window.

When we got back from school Mum said, "There's been a phone call."

"Who from?" we both cried at once.

"I don't know, Mrs. Jones took it, and she didn't note the name."

Mrs. Jones came to clean the house on Mondays and Fridays, because Mum didn't have the time now that she was teaching.

"Oh, for heaven's sake!" cried Fergie, sounding like Dad. "Why not?"

"She said the lady promised to ring again this evening. And one bit of good news, the cheque's come for the first edition; you know, the book at the jumble sale—five pounds."

"Keep it, please," said Fergie. "We owe you and Dad so much."

"Actually I though it might pay for a set of shoes for Ping Pong: her hooves are breaking up a bit," Mum said. "I've rung the blacksmith. He's coming at half-past three tomorrow. I'll hold her until you arrive."

I said, "Thanks a thousand!" and Fergie said, "Great!" and suggested that we had better hurry and change if we were to ride before dark, explaining that he wanted to teach Hopscotch to turn on the haunches. "*And* I've got to drive him into his bridle, so that he stops wandering." Then we ran upstairs with Leerie at our heels.

Tired out by school work and anxiety, we both rode badly, and I quarrelled with Solitaire who didn't like reining-back, because all his schooling to date had been based on going forward into his bridle. After a time he began to rear and then Fergie dismounted and helped me, facing the grey and tapping his legs with a stick. After a time Solitaire began to grasp what was wanted and then Fergie vaulted on to Hopscotch to continue his lessons in opening and shutting gates. At dusk we backed Ping Pong with the felt saddle again and, as she seemed absolutely quiet, Fergie rode her round the village with me at her head, then we schooled Jigsaw, who we had managed to catch this time, until complete darkness.

"No more telephone calls?" we asked as we slammed our homework down on the kitchen table.

"No, you can't do it here. I want it for cooking," Mum said. "Do it in the sitting room or in your bedrooms."

"I just don't understand the maths tonight. They're horrible," said Fergie despairingly.

"It's the teacher's fault. She should have explained them more carefully, that one's a little too vague," said Mum, who had recently been to a parents' evening. "Ask your father when he comes in."

"Dad has no patience. He always shouts," replied Fergie.

"It's only because he gets overtired," our mother said. "Life's such a struggle these days. He doesn't mean to shout." We went into the sitting room and I started to read *Wuthering Heights*, without taking in a word. Then suddenly the phone rang and we both leaped to our feet like a pair of jacks in the box. I got there first.

It was the champion rider of champion hacks.

"My friend, Janet, tells me you have an absolute poppet, a dear little skewbald just right for my little Harvey," she said.

"Oh yes, Tiddly-Winks. She's a good sweet pony," I replied, almost too enthusiastically, making a face at Fergie who was mouthing instructions at me. "She's just right for a very young child."

"I'm sure I want her. I mean, I trust Janet absolutely, but could I just pop over tomorrow and take a look? I'll bring the trailer and then, if she's as good as I'm told, I can bring her back here. Is that all right? Are you sure?"

"What time?" I asked.

"About three?"

"We don't get back from school until around four," I
I explained. "But we'll leave her in the barn, and Mum
will give you the saddle and bridle if you can make it
half-past. Then you can start trying her before we return."

"Oh, that's most sweet of you because I *do* want to get
back before dark," said Angela Calloway. "And don't
worry; Janet has told me the way."

"Great, and thank you," I said.

"See you tomorrow—'bye'."

"Which one, the infant prodigy or the show hack
rider?" asked Fergie.

I told him.

"We may get the money in time to save Patience," he
cried, leaping up and down. "Four hundred or more
pounds could put us in the black."

"Not all," I said, "but most of it, we need five actually."

"Things never come singly," murmured Mum, who was
superstitious. "You'll probably sell three at once."

We went to school with our homework half done and I
hardly attended to lessons, because I was on tenterhooks,
not wanting to part with Tiddly-Winks or Solitaire, and
worrying terribly about Patience.

At ten to four we leapt off our bus at the stop and,
starting to run, I fell over a stone, sprawling across the lane
like a little child.

"Oh, for heaven's sake, are you hurt?" cried Fergie.

"No." I scrambled up and wiped blood from a grazed
knee and the palm of my left hand. "Not much. Come
on!"

We found Mrs. Calloway leading Tiddly-Winks round
the yard with a sweet little curly-haired boy in the saddle.

"Don't they look *the* perfect pair?" she cried. "I must
have her. Janet said four hundred, is that all right?"

We hesitated. "Well, she's only four and a half and she
may grow a little and she needs a little more training.
You've done very well, and I do congratulate you, but

she'll need a bit more before she's fit for the ring—don't you agree?" asked our prospective buyer.

"Of course." I looked at Fergie, who said, "Yes, fine, fine."

"I think it's fair, don't you?" the show hack lady continued. "Are you quite happy? I promise a good home and, as I hope for more children, she will probably be with us for a long time and then we may breed from her."

Harvey was running his tiny fingers through the skewbald's mane, his large blue eyes looked dreamy and happy. "Nice, nice," he crooned.

"Well, off you come now, sunny boy," said his mother, lifting him from the saddle. "She's better than the old rocking horse, isn't she?"

Presently, while the blacksmith finished shoeing Ping Pong, Mrs. Calloway was writing us a cheque, and then she put knee caps on Tiddly-Winks to protect her on the journey. The skewbald went up into the trailer like an angel, then turned to neigh to her friends, and, seeing her sweet, good-natured face perhaps for the last time, I felt tears pricking behind my eyes.

"She's got lots of room and plenty of straw, and I drive very carefully, so don't worry, and I'll telephone to let you know how she's settled in," said Harvey's mother.

A moment later the trailer was on its way.

"Our first satisfactory sale," said Fergie, looking at the cheque, "and just in the nick of time."

"And dear little Tiddly-Winks walked up into that trailer like a dream," I said. "She was so trusting I wanted to cry."

"Oh, really!" exclaimed Fergie with an impatient wave of a hand.

Then our mother called us to come and hold Ping Pong, who was playing up a bit. "*Or* peel the spuds for supper," she added.

"This one's a bit of a monkey," the blacksmith said in his gentle voice. "Whoa, there, steady, my little sweetheart."

"You don't know anyone who wants to buy any nice ponies, do you?" asked Fergie.

"Not just at present," replied the blacksmith, taking a clench from between his teeth. "The market's always a bit slack in November. Come the spring things will look up again."

"I can't think why you both look so dismal," remarked Mum later when we were all sitting round the kitchen table eating supper. "Things are going so well for you now, and it looks as though you've more than broken even."

"It doesn't look. It is a fact. Two hundred and ten pounds plus four hundred," exclaimed Dad. "Why, they've made a profit. Give the cheque two or three days to clear and hey presto, you've repaid the loan. I do congratulate you both most warmly. I was afraid you wouldn't carry it off and you have."

Fergie looked at me then and I nodded, and he said, "We've bad news, Dad."

"No, what's happened now?"

"Joe O'Rourke is a dealer and we've got to buy back Patience."

"Oh, lord, what nonsense is this?" cried our father. "Not all dealers are bad."

"But Jake says . . ." I began.

"Jake dramatises things. He is blessed with a vivid imagination," said our mother.

"She will go for meat," said Fergie, with a catch in his voice. "I'm going to ring Enquiries and find his number. There can't be many of his name in Herefordshire."

"But you can't sell a horse and then buy it back the next day," objected Dad.

"Oh yes you can," said Fergie grimly.

"You're being neurotic," said Dad. "Imagining things. You're overtired."

"No, I'll do it now, if you'll excuse me," said Fergie, looking at least eighteen as he rose from the table, with his lean face very stern and a faraway look in his eyes, as

111

though he was already seeing Joe O'Rourke coming to the phone somewhere in Herefordshire.

"Does that mean you won't be paying all the money back within the time limit, then?" asked Dad, his voice suddenly disapproving.

"I don't know. It all depends, doesn't it?" I said.

"But you must," insisted Dad. "You have put your name to a legal document promising to do so, and I've stood as a surety."

"We've received six hundred and ten pounds," I said, wearily. "Two hundred and ten has been paid back, which leaves us with two hundred and ninety to pay, so if we keep to our agreement, we shall have one hundred and ten pounds left."

"You can't let down Mrs. Wellbeloved, even if it means one pony goes to a doubtful home," Dad told us. "She was so relieved this morning when I put those notes into her hands, her eyes filled with tears of relief. And she still has other bills to meet which are being handled by her lawyer."

"We've been fools," I said, "utter fools. What dreadful mistakes can be made in the space of a moment."

"If you will forgive me saying so," Mum put in, "I do think you are making something of a mountain of what could well be a wee molehill. There's no reason to believe that the dealer hasn't a good home waiting for Patience. Lots of perfectly decent people buy from dealers."

"He's notorious," I said.

"He's still got her," said Fergie, coming back. "He seems to have forgotten all about the Cotswold people. I think he invented them as he went along. He swears he will sell her to a child who wants to go far, but I don't believe him. I spoke to his wife first, and she said her son had taken a truckload off yesterday morning. When I asked where to, she became cagey. I'm sure they were off to the slaughterhouse on the Continent. She would only say Bristol."

"Did you fix anything, then?" I asked.

"Well, he wouldn't really listen to my proposition that we might buy back. He sort of laughed it off. He said that with a bit more schooling she would be worth four hundred and we wouldn't want to raise that sort of money."

"You sold her too cheap," said Dad.

"Thanks for stating the obvious," replied Fergie, looking bitter.

CHAPTER SIXTEEN

YOU'VE DIDDLED MY CHILDREN

We felt dreadful the next morning, while Dad was singing, being glad to pay our cheque from Mrs. Calloway into the bank and to post another from us to Mrs. Wellbeloved's solicitor. Pulling on my school clothes, I realised that our whole pony saving enterprise had filled him with anxiety, because, as our father, he was ultimately responsible for any debts we might incur. Now, for him, the worst was over, but, for us that triumph was tinged with the deepest regret and uncertainty. We had to wait until Saturday and then, by hook or by crook, we were determined to visit Joe O'Rourke's yard and rescue Patience.

"We shall have to advertise again," I told Fergie as we walked back from the school bus stop.

"Yes, yes, that's right," he was stroking Leerie who, as always had come to meet us.

Once home, we gobbled some biscuits and schooled Solitaire and Hopscotch until darkness fell. The grey would now lead off on either leg, canter in quite small circles and jump three feet.

"I'm going to include Patience in the advertisement," I said, "because it won't come out for nine days and we shall have got her back by then."

"A bit risky," suggested Fergie.

"But, if we haven't and someone enquires about her, we'll just say she's sold, and that will be the truth."

"O.K., O.K.," said Fergie irritably. "You're good at advertisements, so I'll leave it to you."

"Children, come and lay the table," called our mother from the house.

"When will she learn that we are no longer kids?" asked my brother.

"When we leave home I suppose," I said.

"Oh, by the way, a letter came for you by afternoon post. I forgot to tell you, what with one thing and another," said Mum, dishing out stew with cabbage and potatoes. "Leerie, sit down; your turn will come in a minute."

"Where, where?"

We were both on our feet at once.

"Wait a minute."

"Or is it a bill?" asked Fergie slowly with the wisdom of second thoughts, "or another demand from Mrs. Wellbeloved's lawyer? The idea of that man keeps me awake at night."

"I don't know. It was typed, formal-looking. Now sit down and start to eat while the meal's hot, and I'll find the letter," said our mother.

We both turned at once to do as we were bid and ran into each other.

"Ow!"

"Ouch!"

"Look where you are going—twit!"

"The same to you," I said.

"My head hurts."

"So does mine."

We began to eat the stew, which was flavoured with garlic, tomato purée and various herbs.

"Here." Our mother handed Fergie the long white envelope.

"Me, me!" I cried.

"Wait, child," said my brother in his most irritating voice.

It was from Mr. Cann, offering three hundred pounds for Solitaire subject to him passing a veterinary examination.

"It never rains but it pours," said Mum. "I tell you things come in threes. Another pony will be sold before the week's out."

115

"He's fixed up for the vet to call at lunchtime tomorrow," Fergie said, passing the letter to me. "Can we miss school, Mum?"

"No, I'll pop home from work. You leave Solitaire in the barn. The vet will know what to do."

"You're lucky," I told Fergie. "You still have two ponies. Soon I shall only have Jigsaw left."

"You can take over Ping Pong. She's much too small for me," he suggested.

"Dad says we must advertise again. We have the money to pay now," I said.

"*If* Solitaire passes the vet we can buy back Patience," remarked my brother.

"So you've agreed to accept three hundred pounds?" asked Mum, starting on her stew.

"It's more than we expected," Fergie said. "But it seems Emlyn Jones was accepting far too little. Joe—the horse dealer—made an offer and he agreed, without realising that you must always push the professionals up a bit."

"Horse coping has always been a dirty game," our mother said.

When we had finished eating our pudding, which was treacle tart, I fetched a pencil and paper and drew up a second advertisement.

Patience, lovely brown mare, 13.3, 5 yrs., by Mastermind, promising jumper, I wrote.

"How's that?" I asked, reading aloud.

"*Quiet, good in traffic, kind temperament,*" suggested Fergie.

"Too expensive. We've got to mention the others as well," I said. "More words mean higher costs."

"*Good in every way,*" suggested Mum.

"But that must be put at the end to cover all the ponies; *that* will save money," said Fergie.

After more discussion we settled on the following:

Patience, lovely brown mare, 13.3. 5 yrs., promising jumper.

Hopscotch, dun gelding, 13 hands, 4 yrs., quiet, but needs riding on.

Ping Pong, grey mare, 12.2, 4 yrs., recently backed.

Jigsaw, bay gelding, 12.4, 3 yrs., nice lively ride.

All good, sound, nice-looking ponies, by Mastermind.

Once again we put our telephone number at the end, with Shropshire in brackets and paid by cheque on our pony account.

Then we wrote to Mr. Cann accepting his offer and Mum gave us two stamps. Afterwards, Dad came back from driving two people to visit an old lady in hospital at Ludlow, and said he would post everything the following morning from a central post office and also pay in the cheque for us.

We went to school the next morning with mixed feelings, glad that we had the money but sorry to lose the ponies and still worried about Patience. Just before lunch I was summoned by my year tutor and asked why my work had deteriorated over the last month. I said I didn't know and the tutor, who was a youngish woman with pale spectacles and a double chin, replied that I *must* know. Her hazel eyes stared at me meaningly as she waited for an answer, and I said that sometimes my concentration took a rest. She snapped that I was being frivolous and then asked whether I had a boyfriend. I replied that I didn't want one at the moment, thank you, and was infuriated to find myself blushing. She said lots of girls did have boy trouble at thirteen so I must excuse her for asking, she was only trying to look after my interests. I said yes, of course; it was most kind of her, but I didn't think I would be going out with boys until I was fifteen.

"Well, pull yourself together, because you are a bright girl, and I don't like to see talents wasted through lack of effort," she told me sternly. "I understand your homework has been below standard in all subjects recently, and this is giving cause for concern. You will be starting on your 'O' Level course next year."

I promised to try harder, and escaped.

Solitaire passed the vet's test, and I cried when he went, having become very attached to him. On Saturday we piled into the Mini and Mum drove us the thirty-odd miles to Joe O'Rourke's yard.

We found Patience in an eaten-down field with three thin ponies, nibbling at some rather yellow hay. She whinnied when she saw us and raised her lean head, which had a look of a thoroughbred about it and, although it was in proportion to her body, could well have belonged to a racehorse.

Joe O'Rourke came out of an ugly, red brick bungalow.

"So you want to buy her back, do you?"

"Yes, definitely," said Fergie, setting his jaw.

"What do you want to do that for?"

"We want to be sure she doesn't go for meat," my brother replied, beginning to walk towards the mare.

"Look," said Joe O'Rourke, "I only sell those for meat that I can't sell elsewhere, the animals I can't warrant sound or quiet."

"All right," I said, "but please, how much are you asking?"

"Three hundred," said the dealer.

Mum gasped. "That's God's truth," the man said. "I'm advertising her at that price next week. I could get two hundred and fifty for her for meat."

"So you diddled my children," said Mum, looking very straightfaced and Scottish, with her dark brows knitted and her mouth very tight.

"Children? Why, they're as tall as you, madam. I made them an offer which they accepted. I can't be fairer than that."

"We'll pay you two hundred and thirty pounds. That will cover your expenses, hay, petrol and everything," said Fergie rather loftily, coming back to stand beside us.

"Three hundred is cheap for a mare of that quality," said the dealer. "And horses are my livelihood. You've made a mistake right enough, and we pay and learn from our mistakes in this trade, that's life, isn't it? That's what

118

living is all about. I bought that mare with a view to selling her for three hundred."

"And don't you think ninety pounds profit a bit excessive?" asked our mother.

"No, madam, that's what horse dealing is all about. I might make a loss that size next week, if I pick up a bad 'un."

"You talked about a wonderful home in the Cotswolds," I reminded him.

"Did I? I daresay I did. There are wonderful homes in all sorts of places, and you seemed to want some fairy tale."

"Two hundred and fifty," said Fergie.

"I'm not moving. I've settled my price, take it or leave it," said the dealer, starting to walk back to the bungalow.

"We have the money," I whispered, "and our aim has been to save the ponies, not to make a profit. Morally we are bound to buy her back."

"All right," shouted Fergie, "on condition you deliver her free of charge, because we have no trailer."

"Done," said the dealer, turning back. "Cash?"

"No, cheque," I said.

"You sold her for cash, so you buy her back for cash," said Joe O'Rourke, his sharp, beady eyes looking straight at us.

"Income tax dodge," murmured our mother. "You can draw the cash from the bank, or rather Dad can. Why not pay on delivery?"

"All right," said the dealer. "Agreed." His eyes softened a little. "And just remember, if you're going into the horse trade, you've got to have your wits about you. There's no room for sentiment. I know where you got those ponies from. Knew as soon as I saw them in your barn, and you've not done too badly for beginners. But you still have a lot to learn."

So Patience came home again, and we groomed her and

petted her until she shone like dark oak and looked like a pedigree dog who knows he is cherished.

The weekend was hectic, for our second advertisement seemed to arouse greater interest than the first had done. There were thirty-two telephone calls, and although most of these were from young girls who wanted beautiful ponies for only one hundred pounds or so, three families arrived on Saturday to see Ping Pong, Patience and Jigsaw. Patience behaved well, but Hopscotch was nappy and the two smaller ponies seemed nervous of strange riders. We had to admit that Ping Pong needed an experienced rider who would school her, and that Jigsaw was still inclined to shy.

Then, towards evening, a mousy-haired, blue-eyed boy came with his parents in search of a gymkhana pony, and took a great fancy to Patience.

"She looks so dark and wild, something out of the woods," he said.

"Try her," said Fergie, turning to fetch the saddle. "Try her in the fields and over the three jumps we have."

The boy, whose name was Terence, helped my brother to bridle Patience and very soon the brown mare was going through her paces. She looked happy to be back and jumped superbly.

"She's fantastic," said Terence. "Just the job for the Prince Philip Cup!"

"She's certainly got a turn of speed," said Fergie, beaming, "although we haven't taught her to bend or anything."

"But she's so handy, and she answers to the leg so well," said Terence, patting Patience enthusiastically. "I'm glad she's used to people vaulting on. I never mount the proper way, it's so boring."

"Right!" said Fergie. "And Patience always waits until you've got your leg over the other side. She's a kind mare."

The parents, a middle-aged couple well wrapped up in overcoats, scarves and boots, smiled.

"Good, then," Terence's father said. "We've looked at dozens. Thank the Lord we've found something to fit the bill at last. The lad's determined to get to Wembley and the finals of the Prince Philip Cup, and where there's a will there's a way. How much are you asking?"

We said three hundred pounds, but Terence's father said he couldn't rise to that, and turned his back as though to walk away.

I said she was worth two hundred and fifty pounds just for meat, and then Fergie, who had taken a liking to Terence, wanted to know how much the parents were willing to offer, and eventually the father said two hundred and fifty pounds, and, to my surprise, Fergie accepted this without quibble. Terence's father wrote us a cheque and we arranged that Jake should deliver Patience to her new owners early the next week—and then we realised that we didn't have to worry any more, and could even pay back our parents.

"So long as all the cheques are honoured," Dad said, opening a bottle of vintage cider later that evening with which to celebrate.

"Terence's father put his address on the back, and if we don't arrange delivery until Wednesday that should give the cheque time to be cleared," said Fergie, who was beginning to learn about some of the practicalities of buying and selling. "I'm sorry to see Patience go, but I'm sure Terence is the right rider for her. She doesn't like dressage much and loves a good gallop. We shall probably watch her on television competing at Wembley in a year or so."

"Only three to sell now," said Dad, filling our glasses.

CHAPTER SEVENTEEN

THE END OF THE ROAD

My story is nearly over. After the sale of Patience, the pressure was off. We didn't worry so much. The next evening a mother and two children came to see Hopscotch. We told her at once that the dun needed a bit more schooling and was nappy at the gate with beginners but all right with us. And she said she was buying the pony for little Cathy but her elder daughter, Samantha, was capable of dealing with nappiness. This mother, Mrs. Mackie, was obviously knowledgeable. She liked Hopscotch's sensible head, his sturdiness and his hard, sound hoofs which had not yet been shod. "He's a tough little pony," she said. "And we like to ride miles and miles with sandwiches in our pockets. Come on, Cathy, have another go, and use your stick if he tries to stop at the gate, just be firm."

"He'll be all right hacking with other ponies," said Fergie. "He's very good and sensible and doesn't try to rush ahead."

"Cathy's tough at heart, although she looks quite delicate," Mrs. Mackie said. "She'll soon get the better of him. Go on, you naughty pony. Trot on! We have two others, one for Samantha, one for me, so he won't be lonely."

Mrs. Mackie had read about our campaign in the newspaper.

"You've done a wonderful job," she said.

"Well, not really," I put in. "One pony got tangled up with a truck and we've concentrated too much on the two larger ones to the detriment of the little ones."

Mrs. Mackie said that there were only nine hours of daylight out of twenty-four and, what with school and all, we must have found it hard to give the time needed. Then she said she was really looking for a reasonably inexpensive pony. "We have our own fields, so fodder is no problem, but I'm divorced and short of capital. Would you consider a ridiculously low offer?"

Fergie and I looked at once another.

"You paid six hundred for the lot," the woman went on, "and this was one of the smaller ones, so would you take one hundred and fifty pounds in three instalments?"

"Instalments?" echoed my brother.

"Fifty pounds now, fifty in December and fifty in January. Does that sound too awful?"

"Not really," I said, patting Hopscotch's creamy dun neck. "He was the third smallest, actually."

"Have you bought in plenty of hay?" asked Fergie, trying to be practical.

"Made our own," said Mrs. Mackie with a note of pride in her voice. "Look, why don't you come and see the place, if you're worried?"

"Isn't there a thing called a banker's reference or something?" asked Fergie at last. "Perhaps if there is we should have one."

"Right. I can see you are a business man. Will do," said Mrs. Mackie, screwing up her freckled nose.

"He will have a lovely orchard and a friend called Dandy, a golden chestnut," said Samantha.

"And a dog and a cat," added the little girl, Cathy.

"Fine. What about transport then?" asked Fergie, still wondering whether he had been awful to ask about the reference.

"Well, do you think you could hack him over, perhaps next Saturday? That will give you time to clear my cheque, and we had better have an exchange of letters about the arrangements."

"The instalments?"

"Yes, that's right," replied Mrs. Mackie, patting Hopscotch. "He's just the sturdy sensible little pony I've been wanting. He was all right leaving the gate with Samantha.

Cathy just needs a little more confidence and determination."

We said we would be glad to bring him over, and then, after she had gone, we went in to tell our parents.

"It's a knowledgeable home," I said.

"Good heavens! You have done well," said Dad, peeling potatoes for supper. "Lend me a hand, will you?"

With the others sold, we were now able to concentrate on Jigsaw and Ping Pong who were not yet quiet enough to be recommended for small children to ride. We began to look at them with new eyes. The bay was brisk, well set-up with rather a high crest for a gelding and a merry air. He had very sharply pointed ears and large eyes in a slightly dish face. Ping Pong was, of course, equally pretty and with rocking-horse dapples and a well-rounded rump. She looked as though she would make an excellent brood mare. Both were now very furry in their winter coats.

"Maybe we should wait until the spring before selling," Fergie said.

But he had reckoned without Jake, who came up the next evening to see how we were getting on.

"You've been champion," he announced, sitting on a bale of straw in the barn. "I never thought you would do it."

"I don't see why not," argued Fergie, looking as though he had never felt a moment's anxiety.

"And I can help you out with the remaining two," Jake went on. "Seeing they are a bit on the small side for you, and Fergie's working for examinations *and* you've got your own ponies to exercise."

"Yes, Silverstar is getting a bit too lively," I agreed. "But how, Jake?"

"Well, it's like this," our friend began, feeling for his matches, then, remembering that he was amongst fodder, putting them back in his pocket. "There's a little girl that trekked with me in the summer—Julie, you may remember her—that wants a pony of her own, but her parents are sceptical. They say it may be just a craze, seeing she was mad on skating, ballet, swimming and the like all in turn and then gave them up."

"Don't we all," I said, "at some time."

"So," continued Jake with a wave of his hand to silence me, "I suggested she borrowed an animal for the winter as a test. If she kept going all through the bad weather, the parents could feel safe in buying her something in the spring."

"And you haven't got a pony to lend yourself?" asked Fergie.

"No, mine are all out now, so I thought of Ping Pong, because Julie's a very nice little rider, sits a treat and yet is always the boss. I reckon she could manage that grey a treat. She's almost twelve, I'm told, but small and wiry, a tough little girl who knows her own mind but is full of commonsense, and she lives only two miles down the valley, so you could keep an eye on things."

"But why not Jigsaw?" I asked.

"I was coming to that," Jake went on. "I've always liked that bay and I'll be happy to buy him from you in the spring, seeing he's sturdy enough for trekking. Meanwhile I'll bring down a few bales of hay to see him through the winter and perhaps you'll ride him now and then, and then every day through March, and I'll have him when he's just coming up for five years old."

"Are you sure?" I asked. "You're not offering just to be kind?"

"No, of course not. I like the pony, and he won't shy trekking because he needn't lead the way unless he wants to. He's got a bit of spirit about him that means he'll go miles without tiring and he'll do a treat for little girls like Julie who want something with just a little bit of extra energy. I don't see Jigsaw ever getting stale and lazy. He's a grand pony and no mistake."

"No, it's not every pony that makes a good trekker," I said. "But I think you're right."

"And I'll give you two hundred pounds at Easter," added Jake.

"Oh, that's too much, especially if you're sending down hay for him," I objected.

"Well, what are you doing with the extra? You've made a tidy little profit, haven't you?"

"We shall be a few hundred up, and we are going to rename the pony account the Save the Ponies Fund, and keep it for emergencies."

"You mean to buy up any pony that needs saving?" asked Jake with his wry smile.

We both nodded. The decision, on the surface so lightly taken, seemed now to add a new purpose to our lives. It was marvellous to think that we would not always have to stand by helpless in the face of suffering and mismanagement. Sitting in the warm barn with the sweet smell of hay around me, the November frost beginning to deck the world with diamonds of frozen dew, I imagined the ponies we might save—skinny, lame and ill-treated, with staring coats and dull eyes, misfits and delinquents in the equine world, waiting to be auctioned, resting weary legs, fearful, unreliable or broken in spirit. I saw our cheque book as their passport to a new and different life. We would fatten and cherish them, retrain and care for them until they were ready to find new and better homes. Many we would save, of course, from the slaughterhouses.

Fergie looked at me and grinned. "Let's wait a bit before we break the good news to Dad," he said.

PONIES IN PERIL

Diana Pullein-Thompson grew up in Oxfordshire in a family of
four children. They all learned to ride when they were very
small, and their first mount was Countess, a retired polo pony,
whom they used to climb on to by stepladder. Diana left school
at fourteen, and, with her two sisters, started the Grove Riding
School, which inspired some of her early books and eventually grew
into a large establishment with forty-two horses and ponies.
She has written over twenty books, and her sisters, Christine and
Josephine, are also well-known as children's writers. She is
married to art historian and museum director, Dennis Farr, and
they live in Warwickshire with their two children, two dogs, a grey
mare called Bianca, and a hamster.